THE FLOODWOOD CHRONICLES

The Wolf of Amalfi

THE FURTHER ADVENTURES OF ARTEMIS FLETCHER

Pete Kennedy

www.highpointlit.com

This edition published by Highpoint Lit, an imprint of Highpoint Executive Publishing.

For information, write to info@highpointpubs.com.
First Edition

ISBN: 979-8-9879203-7-4
Kennedy, Pete
The Wolf of Amalfi: The Further Adventures of Artemis Fletcher

Summary: In *The Wolf of Amalfi* a global adventure of thievery and espionage meets the supernatural. Artemis Fletcher and her intrepid sidekick Ayotunde Ibukun hold down day jobs as respectable college professors, but once out of the classroom they pursue their real vocation as international secret agents charged with an almost impossible task. From a haunted castle in Ireland to the deep forests of Nigeria, the sun-drenched lemon groves of Italy and the jazz clubs and dive bars of 1960s Greenwich Village, they track down and do battle with art thieves. Along the way they team up with shape-changers, engage in sword fights and motorcycle chases, ultimately pursuing a time-traveling pirate up the Hudson River in a breathless climax.
– Provided by publisher

ISBN: 979-8-9879203-7-4 (paperback)
Library of Congress Control Number: 2023912056
Cover illustration by Jennifer Lenox, Vermont artist
Cover concept by Maura Kennedy
Interior design by Sarah M. Clarehart

CONTENTS

ACKNOWLEDGMENTS

I'd like to thank the following people for making this book possible: Maura Kennedy, Diana Ward Powell, Nanci Griffith, John and Suzy Allman, Allan Pepper, Rita Houston, and Vin Scelsa. At Highpoint Lit, thanks to Michael Roney, Sarah Clarehart, Lori Paximadis, and Kendra Millis.

INTRODUCTION

"Artemis, you've been asking me all day for a clue as to your mission here. In fact, you had the clue in your possession when you landed in Rome. The invitation was to speak about the wolf man, the Lycanthrope of Ravello, correct?"

"Correct. The legend, or perhaps an ancient allegory."

"It was neither."

He turned to face her, and once again she recognized the eyes, the yellowish tint when the moon was full. She silently warned herself not to recoil when he leaned in and whispered.

"Artemis, the wolf is back."

PART ONE

THE TWO-HANDED SWORD

CHAPTER 1

THE TEAM

Final exams were a busy time on the Sarah Lawrence campus. Artemis Fletcher was spending more and more time between classes with a new faculty member. A kindred spirit and a fellow adventurer, Ayotunde Ibukun's ambition was to raise awareness and generate enthusiasm in her students by sharing her interest in the deep, unexplored richness of her African Yoruba ancestry. The entire year of 1965 seemed to fly by as they plotted innovations to the campus curriculum, planning ways to best use the Van Leer scholarship endowment. By the end of semester break in January 1966, Ayotunde had taken up residence at Atalanta, and Artemis began initiating her into the life of a moonlighting secret agent. As the spring semester came to a close, they were both tapped for membership in the newly rejuvenated Strabo Society.

The society, named for an ancient Greek geographer, was founded in the early twentieth century as a fraternal lodge for explorers. The initial mandate was to encourage and support discovery, and to further the understanding and appreciation of world culture and history. Sadly, that noble quest gradually devolved into outright thievery. Under the corrupt leadership of Duncan Sinclair and Charles Iverson, the Strabo Society became a global web that illegally enmeshed and stashed away priceless antiquities and artworks. Eventually the ethical downward spiral led to the murder of a young scientist, Alistair Wulver, who mysteriously reanimated as a werewolverine, and the society's web began to unravel. The nefarious network finally collapsed in 1963 when Artemis, who had done legitimate contract work for Strabo, got wind of the society's dark side and formed an alliance with Wulver. She brought her temerity, relentless detective work, and mastery of a range of unusual weaponry to bear and, narrowly escaping assassination, brought down the criminal edifice.

By 1966, the club had survived the maelstrom of Sinclair's and Iverson's criminal indictments and was setting a new course for the future. Kevin Macduff had been a young detective in 1963, working for the society. He narrowly survived an encounter with Wulver-as-wolverine and underwent a personal transformation after the attack. Like Artemis, he saw Strabo in the harsh light of its criminal reality, and he vowed to bring about change. He spent a year on his uncle's upstate farm, baling hay and thinking deeply about the wolverine incident, an experience with nature that went beyond the boundaries of science. The seasons went by, and the following autumn, once the harvest was in, he returned to New York and rejoined Strabo. His goal was to bring the bruised institution back to integrity. The older members embraced his enthusiasm, and he was easily elected director.

One of Macduff's first acts in office was to nominate Artemis and Ayotunde as the club's first female members. They traded their jeans and flannel shirts for formal gowns to attend their investiture at the club. Macduff, dressed in white tie and tails, was the master of ceremonies. He grinned as he strode to the podium.

"Congratulations on this great occasion!"

The Strabo Society membership rose as one to applaud their two newest members.

"Professors Fletcher and Ibukun have distinguished themselves at Sarah Lawrence, and they continue to contribute important research in the fields of history and anthropology. I have no doubt that our titular founder, Strabo the geographer, would have learned much from their published articles, had they been available to him in the first century BC!"

Laughter and more applause.

"And I am particularly proud to introduce them as the first female members in the forty-eight-year history of the society."

Another standing ovation.

After the ceremony, Artemis and Ayotunde sat with Macduff in his office.

"I don't mind telling you both that it's a miracle the society survived the debacle when Sinclair and Iverson went down. The publicity about their global art thievery was nearly fatal to our endowment, but we've turned things around. It's a new day here. Transparency, education, outreach, the end of the Ivy League old boy clique…we'll be looking to both of you for leadership going forward."

Macduff took a sip from his coffee cup.

"Artemis, your friendship with Wulver taught us all something about our relationship with nature. We're not in charge. There is an entire body of knowledge that's still beyond our grasp. Wisdom in the shadows, barely visible, labeled as occult, magic, wizardry. I see my job as trying to unlock those secrets. I feel strongly that the club's real mission is not just to explore but to cast a glimmer of light on that mysterious world."

"It's an honor to be here, Kevin. As you recall, five years ago we wouldn't have been allowed in the door, except for the fund-raising dinner."

"Well, you are indeed here now, and here's what I need you to do for us. I have you both booked on TWA out of Kennedy Airport on Sunday night, the red-eye. By trade agreement, flights from the US have to land first at Shannon in the west of Ireland. From there, you'll connect on a puddle jumper over to Dublin. A driver will transport you to Blooms Hotel in Temple Bar. Take Monday to relax but be down in the pub at eight p.m. Your contact is Shane Whelan. He'll fill you in on the assignment. Shane is a junior professor of Irish folklore and mythology at Trinity College. That's all I can tell you now."

He handed Artemis a manila envelope containing the itinerary and tickets.

"On a final note, no need to bring a crossbow on this trip. You'll be provided with whatever weaponry you need."

Macduff rose and shook both of their hands.

"I am really excited about the future of the society with both of you as members. My goal is that we'll be known for preserving world heritage, not plundering it. You two are valued allies in that quest."

He drained his coffee cup and cast a faux-furtive glance around.

"To be honest, the older members who hibernate in the library, speaking in hushed tones, are not exactly ideal candidates for a dangerous mission. I'm afraid we've been known as a sedentary hermetic lodge, but with you two on board, I think that's all about to change."

CHAPTER 2

THE HA'PENNY BRIDGE

At nine p.m. on Sunday night, Artemis was filling in the *New York Times* crossword puzzle, while Ayotunde scanned their cavernous surroundings. The ultramodern TWA Flight Center was designed like a huge bird in flight. Ayotunde listened to the distant, echoing voice as departures were called, wondering quite literally what tomorrow might bring. As a newly minted secret agent, she was adjusting to the fact that information was doled out in a trickle, and she was astonished that Artemis would simply throw a few things in a duffel bag and take off around the globe with only a plane ticket and the location of an assignment. Artemis assured her that their contact would fill them in when they arrived, but Ayotunde couldn't help but wonder if the mission was simply to retrieve a work of art or if it involved dealing directly with criminals. Macduff had told Artemis that she would be supplied with any weaponry she might need. That was something to ponder as they boarded the Boeing 707.

In her comfortable first-class seat, Ayotunde relaxed as Julie Andrews sang "The Hills Are Alive" on the movie screen. She dozed off to the sounds of the von Trapp family, and when she woke the sun was pouring in the cabin windows. Thirty thousand feet below, she could make out waves crashing on the rocky west coast of Ireland.

The two women spent Monday wandering the lanes of Temple Bar, the bohemian district of Dublin, populated with Trinity College students, street corner poets, and musicians. The narrow streets were like a Tunisian bazaar, a honeycomb of tiny shops selling silk scarves, velvet capes, and hand-sewn bell-bottom trousers. In the balmy June weather, goods were hung on racks outside the shops. American Levi's jeans and leather jackets were premium items, and hit songs imported from the States and England wafted from transistor radios, creating an aural montage as the two women strolled Anglesea Street.

They soaked it all in and spent a bit too much of their Strabo per diem on the latest mod trends. Ayotunde acted as Artemis's fashion consultant.

"Fletch, your leather jacket is great, but you can't dress like Marlon Brando every day. We have to get you in some colorful threads, girl!"

An hour later, Artemis walked out of Arnott's with a shopping bag full of Carnaby Street's latest: corduroy bell-bottomed trousers, a paisley kaftan, and a flowered miniskirt.

"Fletch, if you insist on being blond and slender, you should at least dress like Twiggy!"

"Tunde, I have absolutely no idea who Twiggy is, but I'm putting my wardrobe in your capable hands."

At the Ha'penny Bridge, where the River Liffey divides the bohemian Temple Bar district from the bustling shopping precinct around O'Connell Street, they stopped to watch the throng of pedestrians hurry past. Ayotunde grew reflective.

"You know, Fletch, I've been holding down the fort back in Valhalla while you go off on your assignments. This time, I'm up for the adventure, but I have to admit to a little trepidation. We're a long way from Westchester County. As much as I'm loving Dublin, I don't even know what our job is here."

Artemis chuckled.

"Tunde, you'll get used to that. The Strabo Society doesn't give you details in advance. Once you get to the site, you're plunged right into the deep end. As far as anyone in Ireland knows, we're just two American college professors doing some academic research."

"That's all I know too!"

"Let's see what we find out at the pub tonight. Hey look, there's a shop selling real cable-knit sweaters. We can use those back in Valhalla."

"If we *get* back to Valhalla!"

CHAPTER 3

THE IRISH ASSIGNMENT

Shane Whelan was already seated at the bar when the two women made their way downstairs at Bloom's to the Vat House Bar. He called to the bartender.

"Niall, three pints of Guinness! We'll take them in the snug, and please, no disturbance for a half hour or so."

He beckoned for Ayotunde and Artemis to follow him into a cozy side chamber lined in oak.

"So, we meet! All three of us freed for a few precious months from wearing gowns and dropping occasional quotes in Latin. I understand you are kindred spirits, professors of history and culture, explorers of little-known territory in the intellect and across the globe. Welcome to Dublin and Temple Bar. It was my hope that I could take you round the Trinity College library to show you the Book of Kells and our ancient harp, but I fear there isn't time for tourism. We have a bit of a crisis going on."

"We're ready to get to work, professor, as soon as we find out what the work is."

"First things first. In the classroom I'm called professor, but here in the Vat House, I'm Shane. As a student of mythology, I must tell you, Miss Fletcher, that your article in the journal *Nature* on your experience with Alistair Wulver, the lycanthrope, was my most fascinating reading of 1964."

"It was an enlightening experience, that's for sure."

Whelan became pensive. He took a sip from his pint glass.

"Right, then. The assignment. We at Trinity are deeply concerned about my senior colleague, Dr. Lorcan Foley. He's the college's full professor of Irish folklore and myth, my own adviser during my graduate studies. He's a brilliant scholar with an unrivaled depth of knowledge on the subject, but we fear he may have gone dangerously, as we say, 'round the twist.'"

A fiddler began tuning up in the main room. His plucked open strings E, A, D, and G signaled the start of a session in the Poet's Corner. Whelan continued.

"During the semester just completed, Doctor Foley began to act strangely. He insisted that students and faculty address him no longer as Lorcan Foley, but as Conor Cullin. I asked him in private to enlighten me, and he said he had discovered that he was the reincarnation of our mythical hero, Cú Cuchulainn."

Whelan used the modern pronunciation "Cullin."

"He was convinced that he had encountered the Tuatha Dé Danann, our race of ancient beings, who took him to the Otherworld and gave him special powers, the war-making powers of Cuchulainn."

Whelan took another sip while he let that sink in.

"He became more and more obsessed with the ancient story of the crow, the snow, and the blood."

"Go on."

"It's what we folklorists call a 'grateful dead' story. A wanderer named Jack encounters a dead man who has not been given a proper burial, denying him full entrance to the Otherworld. The corpse revives, in a ghostly state, and offers to grant the living man any wish if he will take care of the internment, assuring Jack that he possesses the 'old knowledge.' They depart on a journey to find certain magic talismans that will win Jack a princess whose hair is black as a crow, skin as white as snow, and cheeks blood red. At the first castle, the servant wrestles with a giant and wins the cloak of darkness, which can render him invisible. This gives him an advantage at the next castle, where he fights another giant and wins the sword of light. Armed with these weapons, they proceed to the third castle, where they descend into the Otherworld and rescue the princess, who is under a demonic spell. Needless to say, a cloak of darkness and a sword of light would be powerful weapons indeed, wouldn't you agree?"

The fiddler started playing "Morrison's Jig" in the next room.

"Well, Professor Foley, who is now convinced he is the warrior Cuchulainn, is fixated on finding those two talismans and assuming magical powers. He is also convinced that he has visited the island abode of Scáthach, the warrior woman who taught Cuchulainn the *cleasa*, certain combat moves that would make him invincible, including the 'salmon leap,' the ability to juggle the sword, dance in midair, and wield the magical spear known as Gae Bolg. Miss Fletcher, if I recall your Wulver article correctly, you have some experience with magic spears."

"That Iroquois spearhead was more of a talisman than a weapon."

"In this case, it's a weapon. It's that weapon combined with his knowledge, the old knowledge from the myths, that make him dangerous. He believes that he really has these powers, and that with the right magic objects he can possess even greater powers. His belief is that he has been chosen by the Tuatha Dé

Danann to bring back the ancient clans and become the warrior chieftain of all Ireland."

"There is nothing more dangerous than delusion, but past experience prompts me to ask, what if he really *does* possess those powers?"

"That's why I asked Macduff to send you both here from New York. We can't go to the Garda, our national police, with this. They would laugh. This needs to be taken seriously. Foley is a charismatic figure, and as Cuchulainn he takes on the charisma of a mythical hero. I shudder to think of the threat to our democratic republic if he's seen as more than just a harmless lunatic."

Ayotunde hadn't touched her Guinness. Her eyes, fixed on Whelan, narrowed.

"Is he here in Dublin?"

"No. He was last spotted in the library at St. Brendan's College in Killarney, down in the Southwest. He asked the clerk for information on Ross Castle."

Ayotunde nodded slowly.

"Our assignment then, is to track him down."

Whelan finished his pint.

"Get some rest. We'll meet tomorrow at noon at Bewley's tea house on Grafton Street, and I will fill in the details as I know them."

CHAPTER 4

GRAFTON STREET

Whelan ordered black tea. Artemis and Ayotunde, still battling jet lag, ordered Bewley's strong house-roasted coffee. Whelan tore a sheet from his Trinity College notebook.

"Ross Castle was the ancestral keep of a clan chieftain from the fifteenth century. He built it on the shore of a lake so that one side would be unapproachable by foot soldiers. There is a high wall around the main tower, with only one entry gate. I'll draw you a diagram of the tower."

Whelan began to sketch.

"The tower only has one entrance. When you come through the door, you are in a small room, a cage, actually. Access to the rest of the building is through a door on the opposite side of the cage. If it's locked, you don't get in. To make matters worse, there is a 'murder hole' in the roof of the cage, through which the upstairs occupants can attack you in any number of creative ways. If the great oak door closes behind you, you have effectively made yourself a prisoner upon entry into the tower."

He sketched the lowest floor with the enclosed cage.

"Now, being European, I would call this the ground floor, and the one directly above that, the first floor. Since you are Americans, I recall that you would call the lowest floor the first floor, and the next one up the second floor and so on, so I'll use that terminology."

He poured a bit of milk into his teacup.

"Now, the next floor up, the second floor in your parlance, was a storage space. The castle has been abandoned for over a century, but there are furnishings still in this space. It's our belief that certain ancient religious vestments, woven on the continent and decorated with gold, may be hidden there. The third floor was the servants' quarters. More items, dating way back, may be stored there. The fourth floor was the family's sleeping chamber. No one has been up there in decades. The top floor was the private stronghold of the chieftain. There is one stone stairway linking all the levels. On the roof are crenellated battlements, the classic castle rooftop defense."

Whelan put the finishing touches on his sketch.

"The original chieftain was, according to legend, sucked out of an upper floor window and now resides as a ghost at the bottom of the lake. It's a spooky place."

Artemis asked the waitress for a second cup of coffee.

"What's Foley's interest in Ross Castle?"

"One of the legends about the castle is that the magical weapons—the cloak of darkness, the sword of light, and the magic spear—are hidden in plain view in Ross Castle, but visible only to those with the second sight, the ability to see the enchanted world around us. Foley has lectured on this for years in the classroom. Now he's become, in his mind, one of those legendary characters."

Whelan looked down at his teacup, as if to read guidance in the leaves.

"There are many on this island who profess the Christian church but also cling to the old beliefs, the beliefs that grew up out of the ground and still remain hidden in the bogs and under the hills. Walk gingerly in a ruined castle, my friends, or especially an old abbey graveyard. You are not alone."

The three of them finished their beverages silently. Then Whelan spoke in a suddenly jovial voice.

"Well, that's sorted out. Now, who here has experience driving on the correct side of the road, not wrong way round, like you do in the States?"

Both women raised their hands.

"Excellent! There will be a hire car waiting for you at Bloom's in the morning. Before we part ways, I invite you to come have a look at certain treasures that we have locked away on campus."

Whelan led the way down Grafton Street to the gates of Trinity College. At a nondescript storage building he unlocked a padlock and swung aside a heavy oak door. He shone his flashlight along the back wall and it flashed silver like a salmon stream. Swords, dozens of them, hung there.

"Now, to flesh out your mission, our hope is that you will locate the professor and find out what, if any, ancient relics he actually has in his magical arsenal. If he has a cloak, a sword, and a spear, they need to be brought here to the university to be evaluated and safely stored. As you might guess, there is the slight issue of the professor himself. We know he's gone round the twist; we're just not sure of how far round the twist."

"So he could be violent?"

Whelan sighed and pointed at the row of swords.

"For better or for worse, our history is one of conflict, and thus we have no shortage of antique weaponry in our archive.

Most of these are of the old Irish two-hander style, but I have one here that might interest you."

He opened a cedar chest lined in red velvet. Inside lay a sword with a two-foot-long curved blade, quite unlike the Irish straight-bladed swords. Artemis looked at the sword, then at Whelan.

"A Samurai katana sword. Beautiful! Looks like original fifteenth century."

"Exactly, but of course you would recognize that, having trained in the dojo in Kyoto."

"How do you know that? I've never written that up."

"Research is my job. Now, this piece. It was given as a gift in 1920 to our national poet William Butler Yeats. A Japanese gentleman by the name of Junzo Sato heard him read in the US, and he was so moved that he decided to convey this precious family heirloom to Yeats. It's still in the family, temporarily on loan to Trinity."

"'Sato's gift, a changeless sword'—I recall that line from Yeats. May I try it out?"

"You may have a chance to do more than that in Killarney. It will be in the rear compartment of your hire car in the morning. If you get stopped by the Garda on your way west, tell them you need it for your academic research. And for you, Ayotunde."

He unsheathed another blade, shorter but equally sharp and menacing.

"Your skean. It's our traditional dagger."

She gulped.

"Okay then. My first dagger."

She threw a glance in Artemis's direction, with a raised eyebrow.

Shane continued. "Now, as I said, the tower is five stories tall, and it's surrounded by a high stone wall. There may be some climbing involved. Have either of you done any rock climbing?"

Artemis grinned. "I did a bit of scree scrambling in the Himalayas a couple of years back."

"Well, this won't be like trekking on the roof of the world, but you will need to be kitted out. I contacted the IMC, the Irish Mountaineering Club, at their hut in the Burren region. Fantastic limestone climbing out there. They agreed to drop a haul bag of essentials for you at the hotel in Killarney."

"You mean we don't just ring the doorbell and wait for Foley to invite us in?"

"If he does, you can consider that like a spider inviting you into his web."

As they walked across the campus, Whelan pulled Artemis aside and spoke softly.

"Artemis, your official Strabo mission is to locate the antiquities and get them here to the college, but I must ask you another favor. We need to get Professor Foley back on campus. If he's holed up in a ruin in the West, we can't just leave him there, thinking he is the hero Cuchulainn. He needs to come back to Dublin and get psychiatric treatment. I fear that he's never going to do that on his own volition. Do you get my drift?"

"Got it."

The three of them reached the college gate. Whelan tipped his tweed driving cap.

"Good luck finding Professor Foley, or Cuchulainn, as the case may be…"

He lit a Galois, shook the match, and tossed it.

"And even better luck when you do."

CHAPTER 5

INTO THE WEST

In the morning, a Morris Minor Traveller, complete with wooden side panels, was waiting for them in front of the hotel. Once outside of Dublin, the two-lane roads were narrow all the way across to Limerick, and they got narrower as the pair bore south-west toward Killarney. There they planned to throw their duffels in a hotel room and head straight to the castle.

South of Limerick, they couldn't resist stopping to hike through the ruins of an abandoned medieval abbey. In the mist, the old stone walls looked like a soft-focus photograph. They walked through a courtyard and into the roofless nave of what was once the chapel. They found themselves whispering as a sort of reverence settled over them. They were jolted out of their reverie when they heard voices just outside the church walls.

A young man was leading an elderly woman by the arm as she gestured around the ruins.

"This was the chapel. Yes, yes."

She caught sight of Artemis and Ayotunde.

"Oh, visitors! Isn't it lovely here. Sad and yet lovely. Let me show you something, my ladies, out in the courtyard."

She led the way, with the young man holding her arm and the two women following. The old woman pointed down at the rough-hewn stone terrace.

"Under these stones, the nuns were buried for two centuries. Holy women, who spent their lives cloistered in silent prayer, in this lonely spot. Holy women, yes. God be with us."

She glanced around.

"They left no markers when they went to our Lord, but I can tell you where each one is buried. Each and every one."

They stood silently for a few minutes, and then Ayotunde thanked the elderly woman.

"This has been great. We're history students from America. Could we take a photo with you?"

Ayotunde handed her Polaroid Swinger to the young man, and the two women stood smiling on either side of the fragile elderly lady. Then it was time to get back on the road.

Artemis turned the ignition key but let the Morris idle while Ayotunde carefully tended to the Swinger. It was a cute, friendly looking camera, made for grabbing quick snapshots, but it was finicky. The Swinger carried its own developing chemistry, eliminating the need to wait for prints from a lab, but to use it required a bit of choreography, pulling a tab while pressing a button with pinpoint timing and pressure. That bit of choreography, if successfully executed, would release a single sheet of print paper along with a companion sheet of developing reagent, bound in a sort of chemical sandwich. Once in the open air, it was only a matter of seconds before the user could pull the sandwich apart, revealing the photo. Ayotunde was skilled at the art. Once she had deftly pulled the sandwich out of the camera, Artemis put the car in gear and steered south toward Killarney.

Ayotunde's eyes widened when she peeled the final print off the reagent sheet.

"Oh my gosh. Fletch, pull over. I want you to see this."

The photo was clear and precise in detail. It was a picture of Ayotunde and Artemis standing on either side of a smiling young woman who couldn't have been more than twenty-five years old. They were both quiet as Artemis pulled the Morris Minor back onto the two-lane road. Artemis glanced over at Ayotunde, and they both shook their heads slowly. Whelan was right. They were not alone in the old graveyard. Driving into the West was beginning to feel like entering a realm where the rules of everyday life no longer applied. Next stop, the Great Southern Railway Hotel, and then on to Ross Castle.

CHAPTER 6

THE CASTLE

Ross Castle was owned by absentee landlords. It sat unoccupied and closed off to visitors on the grounds of Killarney National Park. As Ayotunde and Artemis hiked in, they were treated to views of Ireland's tallest mountains, purple sandstone ridges with evocative names: the Reeks, the Bones, Eagle's Nest, and Hag's Tooth. The castle stood on the bank of a large lake with dozens of small islands, places where a fugitive could hide a canoe in the overhanging brambles and disappear. The peaks and the lake dotted with islands reminded Artemis of Floodwood, and she wondered about her old friend Wulver's life in the Iroquois Otherworld. She felt drawn back to the Adirondack lake country, but there was a mission to accomplish in Ireland first.

As they neared the castle across a broad meadow, a herd of red deer, elk-like and larger than whitetails, spooked and ran toward the wooded hills. Then two unexpected sights caused the women to pause in their approach: a canoe was tied to an iron ring on the lakeside wall, and the massive front gate of the bawn, the outer wall, was open.

They slowed their pace. If someone was watching from the tower, there was no way they could gain access undetected—in fact, they would have already been seen. Artemis silently gestured to keep going, and Ayotunde nodded in assent. The courtyard gate swung open easily. Artemis half-expected it to slam shut behind them, like a scene from a vintage horror movie, but it hung loosely open, on rusty hinges. They reached the tower door. Ayotunde pushed gently on it, and it too swung open. The women exchanged glances. Of course it was a trap, but they expected a trap, and they hadn't come this far to turn back. They passed through and entered the cage. This time the horror movie played out. The massive oak door slammed shut behind them. In the sudden darkness, they had to feel along the bars of the cage to find the gate that would give them access to the upper floors. It was locked. As their eyes became accustomed to the dimness, they could see that a system of pulleys and thick hemp rope controlled egress from the cage. The pulleys were manipulated from above, and the occupants of the cage were snared like game in a deadfall trap. Their hunter, in the chamber overhead, wasted no time in making his presence known.

"*Céad míle fáilte*, a thousand welcomes, lovely visitors!"

This was followed by maniacal laughter. The women stood frozen. The voice was coming from the level just above them.

"Welcome strangers! My sincere apologies for the decrepit condition of your accommodations. Perhaps a teatime sweet will ameliorate any disappointment."

The trap door over their heads opened, and a white powder rained down on them. They brushed it frantically from their hair and clothing. Chemical warfare in a medieval castle was not on the list of dangers they expected to encounter. Ayotunde, fearless, touched her index finger to her tongue.

"Fletch. This is sugar."

More laughter from above.

"Fáilte, welcome! I hope you have enjoyed my soul cage. Perhaps you will come for high tea and more sweets next time."

The iron gate on the inside wall of the cage creaked upward on rusty chains. The oak front door behind them remained shut, but they were free to leave the inner portal and climb the stairs to the next floor. The ghostly laughter and the rain of sugar had set them off kilter. Being toyed with didn't reassure them that the real danger wasn't lurking on the upper floors.

There was no further sound from above. With no desire to linger any further on the first floor, Artemis and Ayotunde crept slowly up the stone stairs. Daylight was still slanting through the narrow tower windows. There was nothing on the second floor save the half-empty bottom-stitched sugar sack. They continued step by step up the next flight of stairs. At the third floor landing, Artemis caught her breath, then whispered, "Tunde, you have to see this."

An eight-point rack of red deer antlers projected from the round stone wall of the otherwise bare room. On it hung a cloak, a gold-embroidered church vestment. The Flemish-style embellishment, a woven tapestry of a unicorn being speared by hunters, was visibly ancient, but the goldwork glinted brightly in the sunlight.

Artemis whispered, "Let's not touch it. One booby trap per day is sufficient."

Ayotunde raised an eyebrow and nodded in agreement.

"Now, I wonder what's on the upper floors."

They made their way one step at a time up the next stairway. The fourth-floor chamber was also lit by sunlight, which seemed to radiate from the polished blade of an Irish two-handed sword that hung from a second rack of red deer antlers. On the opposite wall was a third rack of antlers, holding a spear. Artemis and Ayotunde looked at each other, wide eyed. Could it be Gae Bolg, the weapon of Scáthach the warrior woman?

"Tunde, is it possible that Foley actually found the weapons?"

"There's still the upper floor and the roof, Fletch. Let's go."

On the top floor, an ash window casement was swinging in the afternoon breeze. Ayotunde rushed across the round chamber and looked down at the lake.

"Fletch, the canoe is gone."

"There's only one egress. The front door that shut behind us on the ground floor. He couldn't have gotten past us undetected unless…"

"Unless he leapt fifty feet down and landed unhurt in a canoe. That's impossible."

"Impossible unless…Tunde…the salmon leap."

"That would mean he really did contact Scáthach the warrior, and she taught him the feats of magic."

"Including the combat tricks, the deadly dancing, and the sword juggling."

"And the cloak downstairs…the cloak of darkness? Fletch, if our mission was just to retrieve the artifacts, we'd be done, but if we have to snare Foley, too, that's a different thing entirely. Is there something you haven't told me yet?"

"Well, there is one more little bit of information…"

"Let me guess. We *do* have to snare Foley."

"Yes, or at least detain him until the Gardae can pick him up and transport him back to Dublin, where he can get a psychiatric evaluation. So, our work is not done here yet. Let's get back to the hotel and pick up the climbing gear. That front gate was left open to lead us into his trap. He toyed with us just long enough to escape. He knows we'll be back, and I don't think he'll be showering us with sugar next time."

Down on the ground floor, the great oak door was once again open. They hiked back to the car in the long summer twilight.

CHAPTER 7

STORMING THE WALLS

Back at the Great Southern, they assembled their kit for the night. They had no intention of entering through the cage again. The plan was to scale the outer wall, then anchor a sling to one of the crenellated battlements on the roof. That would give them climbing access to every level of the fifty-foot tower. They checked the contents of the haul bag.

Sling

Two harnesses

Hex nuts

Chalk

Carabiners

Helmets

Artemis sheathed the katana sword, Ayotunde packed the skean, and they headed back to the castle. At ten minutes before midnight, they were padding across the lakeside meadow in rubber-soled climbing shoes. The canoe was there, tethered to the iron ring, and the front gate was open.

"Looks like the welcome mat is laid out for us."

They crept up to the outer bawn. Artemis attached the hex nut to the sling and threw it over the wall. She pulled it quietly until the hardware caught somewhere in the ancient cracked stone. She pulled harder. It held. She chalked her hands and pulled herself up the wall. Ayotunde followed, using the same line. The top of the bawn was a narrow walkway where the clansmen of yore could shoot arrows or pour boiling oil on unwanted visitors. They caught their breath. Artemis turned on her headlamp and aimed it down at the tower door. From her vantage point it was clear that it had been rigged with a massive oak beam that would fall across the door as soon as it was closed, locking it from the outside. Anyone who chose to pay a visit to Foley would find themself an instant prisoner in the cage. The only way to get in would be to scale to an upper window.

The bawn was high enough that Artemis could attach her rope and harness to the sling with a carabiner and toss it, with the added weight of the hex nut, up onto the roof of the tower. On the third try, the sling and hex caught in a stone crevice on one of the crenellated battlements. She yanked the sling as hard as she could. It held. They swung across to the tower and got their footing, climbing slowly to a second-story window. They waited silently outside for a full five minutes, listening for any sound within. Then Artemis hoisted herself through the narrow window and dropped to the oak floor. Ayotunde followed. They unhooked their harnesses and lay silently, catching their breath again and listening.

Artemis signaled for both to turn on headlamps. In the silent tower, they aimed their lights at the wall where the cloak had hung. It was gone.

With the cloak missing, their prey was not only dangerously insane but also invisible. They crept up the stairs to the third floor. Their lamps reflected off the shining sword blade, where it hung as before on the wall. The game was in Foley's court. As they switched off their headlamps, Artemis gasped. The sword, the mythical sword of light, was still illuminated. Illuminated from within. A voice broke the silence.

"*Failte! Céad míle fáilte*, my lovelies! A hundred thousand welcomes! And now we engage in mortal combat for the soul of Eire!"

The sword appeared to leap from its hanging scabbard. The invisible wielder danced, juggled the weapon, and leapt from point to point in the round chamber. Artemis had just enough time to unsheath the katana before Foley lunged at her. She parried with her dominant left hand, then tried a riposte, but it was impossible to accurately determine where her opponent's body was. He could see all of her, but she could see only his sword, leaving her able to parry defensively but not strike offensively. She tried to lunge, but Foley salmon-leapt to the rafters. There was nothing to do but back off and hope for him to trip up.

She started backing down the steps, mentally repeating Musashi's ancient sword fighting mantra: *balance*. At the landing, Foley lunged again, and Artemis parried, but the sword of light struck with such force that the katana flew from her hand and tumbled down the stone stairway.

Ayotunde shouted from the top of the stairs.

"Fletch! Gae Bolg, the magic spear!"

She tossed the spear past Foley's invisible presence, and Artemis caught it in her left hand. Now it was magic spear against magic sword. Artemis continued backing down to the ground floor, and Foley followed, lunging madly while she parried with the spear. At the bottom of the stairs he gave a mighty lunge. She knew from the arc that it was two-handed, intended to finish off an opponent. She parried and the sword of light severed the spear just below the head. The impact was so strong that she fell backward into the open cage, and the sword followed her in. Foley slashed the rope holding the great oak outer door open, and as it slammed and locked from the outside, the sword of light turned toward Artemis. The tip gently touched her windpipe.

"So sad to have to *cut* your visit short, so to speak."

Ten seconds passed, feeling like ten hours. Then suddenly, the trap door of the murder hole opened and a torrent of white powder poured down on them. A torrent of sugar. Foley's form suddenly appeared, a diminutive white-cloaked snowman. He threw down the sword and bellowed in agony.

"The cloak! You philistines! You've ruined the cloak!"

Artemis grabbed the magic sword, and as she fell backward through the cage door, Ayotunde released the chain pulley on the first floor. The iron bars slammed down.

"Thanks, Tunde! Looks like we'll have to rappel back down from a window. It's a bit crowded on the ground floor."

As they hiked out of the park, they could hear the mad captive shouting.

"Philistines! My spear broken, my cloak ruined, and my sword, my precious sword, stolen!"

In the morning, Artemis put in a call to the Killarney Garda.

"This is Artemis Fletcher. I'm a visiting scholar from Sarah Lawrence College. Yes, New York, that's correct. My associate and I were doing a bit of research at Ross Castle and we discovered a burglar who seems to have somehow ensconced himself in a medieval trap. After you book him, please send his cloak to Professor Shane Whelan at Trinity College. It may need a bit of restoration."

CHAPTER 8

RETURN TO TEMPLE BAR

Back in the snug room of the Vat Pub, Whelan smiled and raised his pint glass.

"Yeats tells us that it's an ancient custom to sacrifice a fish to Artemis, the goddess of the hunt. I hope this basket of fish and chips, wrapped in newsprint, will suffice."

He took his first sip.

"In all seriousness, I express my thanks on behalf of Trinity College. The Irish two-handed sword will go into our collection. The skean will go back into storage, and Willie Yeats's katana? Her battle scars only serve to reveal her true soul. She was wielded in battle on Irish soil. I think the bard would approve.

"It was an honor to hold it, Shane."

"As far as the severed spearhead of Gae Bolg goes…I want you to take it with you.

"Are you sure about that?"

"Those of us who study the old knowledge come to believe certain things. You've witnessed some of those things in the past two days. I can assure you, from my own reading, that these objects only become magic talismans when imbued with power by a wizard like Scáthach, and only in the hands of a student the goddess has trained herself. For that reason, they are harmless now, unless you happen to know, perhaps, a goddess who might reactivate the spearhead's power."

They toasted all around.

Checking out of Blooms, Artemis picked up a letter at the front desk. It was an invitation to lecture at the Castel Nuovo in Naples. The subject would be a legend of local folklore, "The Lycanthrope of Ravello," with lodging provided at the castle itself.

"Hmm…It would be nice to visit an ancient castle and not be attacked by an invisible madman."

Ayotunde grinned.

"It sounds perfect, Fletch. Actually, I've been hoping to make a trek to Nigeria this summer to research my Yoruba culture class. Sadly, the region's not a safe place. There's talk of a civil war coming. I will need to be able to move about and remain inconspicuous."

Ayotunde's dark bronze face turned serious. She continued.

"Look at me, Fletch. Like so many of my brothers and sisters, I can't trace my ancestry further back than 1619, but I know from my culture, and from my beautiful physiognomy, that I am Yoruba. I know it deep in my soul. That's why I'm drawn there."

She relaxed and smiled warmly.

"I wouldn't want to endanger you, and I'm determined to succeed in my first solo mission, if I'm called upon to help out while I'm there. We can reconvene back in Westchester."

"You are ready for that first solo mission. And Tunde, thanks. You saved my life back there in Killarney. I had a magic spear for a weapon and all you had was a knife and a bag of sugar. It was your brilliance and your lightning reflexes that saved the day."

"That skean dagger came in handy after all!"

"Well, you were courageous."

Artemis reached into her duffel bag.

"Tunde. Take this with you."

She pressed the spearhead of Gae Bolg into Tunde's hands.

"It may not be the only magic spearhead in Nigeria, but I'll bet it's the first Irish one, and Tunde…"

She grinned.

"You never know when you might need a little bit of magic!"

PART TWO

The Mask Thief

CHAPTER 9

ABENI

On the eight-hour flight through London to Lagos, Ayotunde chatted with an older woman in the seat next to hers on the VC-10. Her companion introduced herself as Abeni Abiola. She had a broad, friendly face. A mother's face. Tunde liked her immediately.

"Delighted to meet you, Miss Abiola."

"Please, call me Abeni. And you are?"

"Ayotunde Ibukun. I'm a professor at Sarah Lawrence College in the States."

"Wonderful! And what brings you to Nigeria, in addition to your Yoruba name?"

"I'm developing a Yoruba curriculum, a new program to explore the deep roots of our African American culture. I'm sure you know we have a civil rights movement gaining strength in the States."

"Oh my yes. We read all about Dr. King in the Nigerian papers. We follow with the greatest interest. Miss Ibukun, you must come and visit me on campus at the University of Ife.

"You are associated with the university?"

"I curate the museum, darling *omo*. Nigeria can be a dodgy place to travel on one's own. Let me orient you before you head out for your adventure in Yorubaland."

CHAPTER 10

POJU

Ayotunde traveled light. She hand-carried her duffel bag through Lagos customs and immigration. The main concourse was a sea of brightly colored fabric: women wearing *gele* headgear and men dressed in formal *agbaba* gowns. The dizzying variety was like a painting that depicted the panoply of traditional cultures that made up the dense and diverse Nigerian population. She made her way through the crowd to the taxi stand. A loudspeaker was blaring a repeated announcement in English: "Do not accept any ride from a driver who has not been prearranged!"

A whistle-blowing taxi wrangler was keeping order.

"Do you have a driver waiting for you, madam?"

Ayotunde bit her lip. That was a detail she'd forgotten.

At that moment, she heard her name.

"Miss Ibukun, over here, please!"

A young man was standing beside a Volkswagen Beetle. He wore bell-bottom jeans and a T-shirt sporting a graphic image of

Bob Dylan. He held a sign with one word in large handwritten letters: STRABO.

"Miss Ibukun, Director Macduff from the Society wired me in advance of your arrival. He asked that I provide you with transportation in-country. Allow me to confirm my legitimacy. You graduated from Scarsdale High School in 1956, from City College of New York in 1960, and you are working on your doctorate while teaching at Sarah Lawrence College. If that is correct, please jump in so we can get out of this congested area."

Ayotunde nodded and jumped inside, and the VW pulled away from the taxi stand.

"I apologize for the sidewalk testimony, but it is customary here for a chauffeur to assure his passenger that he is the genuine item. I am not actually a taxi driver, though. In reality, I am a teacher at the University of Ife. On campus I am known as Professor Adepoju Oroya, but please call me Poju."

"I gather that Macduff has already told you my full name, but my friends call me Tunde."

"Very well, Tunde. You have already noticed, I'm sure, that most people here in Nigeria speak English. We only gained our independence from Britain a few years ago. At the university and museum in Ile-Ife, we seek to preserve and rediscover our Yoruba culture and heritage. I understand that your destination is the sacred grove of Osun, the river goddess."

"That's correct. I want to study the thirteenth-century sculpture in the Ife museum, as well as the modern art in the grove."

"Lodging has been arranged for you on campus. I have class tomorrow morning. In the afternoon we will travel north to the sacred grove. In the meantime you have an invitation to visit the sculpture gallery at nine a.m. with Dr. Abiola. I believe you know her as Abeni."

Ayotunde smiled.

"So Strabo has spared no details in arranging my trip."

"With all due respect, director Macduff considers you the future of the society. He is very excited about your work."

"I just survived a mad Irish professor with a magic sword, so I'm ready for the next challenge, Poju."

"Very well. We will turn east at Ibadan toward Ile-Ife, in the heart of Yorubaland."

CHAPTER 11

ILE-IFE

Abeni greeted her new colleague warmly.

"Welcome, Ayotunde, to your ancestral home. Before we tour the gallery, come to my office for a cup of tea while we chat. Do you take milk?"

"No, black is fine, thanks."

"We still have so many British customs, even in small things. But you are here to discover Yoruba. Let me give a word of warning, first and foremost. We are a young country, and just as your country had an unstable period when the former colonies struggled to come together as a union, we have entire cultures that existed separately for centuries, until the British drew a line around us in 1800. There are various tribes within those cultures as well. The tragedy of the slave trade set brother against brother, and kings against their own subjects. We still labor under the remnants of that cloud of slavery, just as your own country does. You flew over the Badagry Lagoon on your approach to Lagos. That was the jumping-off point, the end of one's free life. Once you reached the docklands on the other side, you became cargo, and then merchandise. That is, if you survived the crossing."

The two women sipped their tea silently for a few moments.

"Now, let me explain something to you, Ayotunde. We experienced a violent government coup back in January. There is talk on the grapevine, as you say, that another coup is coming any day now, a counterpunch against the first one. I fear that there will be more violence, perhaps even civil war. Hopefully we here in the holy city will be spared bloodshed, and I pray that will be true as well up in Osogbo, where the sacred grove is. Please, *omo*, my child, marvel at the artwork, learn the spiritual practice, bask in the beauty of the song and poetry, and then make your way safely home before violence erupts again. Will you promise me?"

"Of course. Danger is part of my work, but I don't court it foolishly."

"Thank you, Ayotunde. Now, let's look at some sculpture."

They rinsed their teacups and walked toward the gallery.

"The golden age of our art was the thirteenth century. We had a period of social stability before the European ships arrived. Our blacksmiths didn't shoe horses; they created the art you are about to see."

They turned the corner. Ayotunde gasped. She was surrounded by faces—real faces with personalities—in gorgeous dark, deep bronze. She stood silently, looking into the eyes of ancestors from eight centuries earlier. African ancestors from before the Atlantic crossing. She felt a deep spiritual connection, a deep sense of peace.

"These were found in two hoards by construction crews during the colonial period, in 1938 and again in 1957. I will tell you something that we find rather humorous, Ayotunde. The colonial authorities couldn't believe that a 'primitive' culture could have created this beautiful art. They actually tried to argue that the ancient Greeks or perhaps fifteenth-century Italian artists must have visited Yorubaland and left these behind!"

Both women shook their heads slowly.

"Some of these images are of kings, or *oba* as we call them. The others are of *orishas*, helpful spirits. While you are here and up in Osogbo, you will be protected by an *orisha*."

"Maybe she will accompany me back to the US."

"Ayotunde, one result of slavery is that Yoruba culture is an integral thread in the fabric of the so-called New World. Think of modern dance, jazz, blues, rock and roll, gospel music. The people on board the slave ships brought with them the seeds of those art forms, which have now spread around the world. But this art..." She gestured around the gallery. "This is ours. This is the taproot."

As Poju's VW Beetle pulled up in front of the museum, Abeni gave Ayotunde a hug.

"*Omo*, my child, when you reach Osogbo, go to the office of Suzanne Wenger. She is the artist who spearheaded the restoration of the sacred grove. I lunched with her in Paris last week at UNESCO headquarters. She is still abroad, but I wired her yesterday, and she will have her site manager, Keyshia Ojo, show you around and give you the history of the grove. Promise me again that you will be careful, *omo*."

"Of course, Abeni."

Ayotunde climbed into the Volkswagen for the two-hour trip to Osogbo.

CHAPTER 12

KEYSHIA

Keyshia, the site manager, embraced Ayotunde. She was dressed in traditional garb.

"Welcome. Madame Wenger sends her regards from Geneva. She is quite familiar with Sarah Lawrence and the Strabo Society, and she wishes you all the best in your efforts to bring recognition of our great culture to the larger world. Now, blue jeans and a baseball jersey will never do at the grove. We must get you outfitted properly."

Keyshia handed Ayotunde a wicker suitcase and pointed her to an empty office. "Get the basics on and then call me. I will come and sort out the details."

Ayotunde looked at herself in the mirror. *Gele* headwrap, *buba* top, and *iro* sash wrapped around her hand-loomed gown. She felt tears well up as she saw in the mirror a distant ancestor.

"You look fabulous! Now, had you been born here in your homeland, your parents would have gone to the priest, the *babalawo.* He would cast the sacred palm nuts on the divination board and consult with Esu, our god who channels communication with *ifa*, the divine force. The ceremony would reveal your name and give us clues about your future. Now, let us go to the sacred grove."

Before she left the room, Ayotunde glanced once more at her image in the mirror and smiled.

CHAPTER 13

THE GROVE

"We must speak very quietly in this place. Pilgrims come here to worship Osun, the goddess of the river. There are multiple grottos in the forest, dedicated to our goddesses, gods, and *orishas.* Although this is not a tourist attraction, it's a haven for art lovers. Madame Wenger, who was originally from Austria, embraced Yoruba, embraced *ifa*, and pioneered a movement she called "new sacred art." She encouraged regional artists to learn and revive the old techniques, presenting their work in a modern context. Many of the icons we pass will strike you as modern art, but they all have the *ayanmo*, the old life force within."

The two women stopped at art sites nestled in the grove. A number of the works were larger-than-life terra-cotta heads, with realistic faces like the ancient bronze heads in the museum.

"These large heads are our protectors, avatars of the spirit realms. We are coming to an important worship site, the grotto of the goddess Yemoja, the mother of all things."

As they rounded a bend in the path, Keyshia recoiled in dismay.

"No! No, Ayotunde, tell me that this isn't true."

"What is it, Keyshia?

"The mask of Yemoja is gone!"

Keyshia was distraught. They sat on a wooden bench facing the iron stand on which the earthenware mask should have been mounted.

"There is a mystery of late in the grove, Ayotunde. Icons have gone missing, always terra-cotta goddess heads. The strange thing is, two weeks later they have always been replaced, under cover of night. We don't understand why a thief would return a priceless work of art."

"So they don't turn up on the international black market?"

Ayotunde was thinking back to the stories Artemis had told her about the crimes of the old Strabo Society regime.

"The art works come right back to their places, but it's upsetting, and pilgrims have come from all over Yorubaland, all over the global diaspora, to honor them, only to find them gone. Ayotunde, Poju must drive us back to Osogbo, to the *babalawo*. I feel that you have come to solve this mystery. *Opon-Ifa*, the divining board, will tell us."

CHAPTER 14

THE BABALAWO

The priest arranged a smooth surface of sand on the divining board. Two assistants began chanting call-and-response poetry while the *babalawo* beat a rhythm to manifest the presence of Esu, the spiritual interlocutor. Eyes closed, he held sixteen palm nuts in his left hand. As Esu spoke to him, he slid the nuts, one at a time, onto the board. When he removed them, they had created a pattern in the sand of vertical, horizontal, and slanted lines. Ayotunde thought of the patterns of the *I Ching* her teacher Professor Campbell had lectured on. The priest read the pattern and looked up at the two women seated on the mat across from him.

"Your name, Ayotunde, means 'joy has returned.' You were sent here to find your ancestors, but also to help them. Their images are disturbed in the sacred grove. They come and go, which is not like the gods. The thief is here in Osogbo. You are here to restore stability to the grove. Esu says that you have resolved mysteries before. If you help us, joy will return, Ayotunde."

"*Babalawo*, I have a favor to ask."

He nodded.

"This..." She took the spearhead of Gae Bolg from her backpack.

Keyshia raised an eyebrow and silently mouthed the word *Irish*.

"This was given to me in case I needed an extra bit of *orisha* assistance."

The priest smiled and held the spearhead. The drummers resumed their hypnotic rhythm. The *babalawo* held his eyes closed. His lips moved silently. After a few moments he gestured to his fellow priests to fall silent.

"Esu gave me one more word from the *ifa*. I don't know why but I must give it to you. It is *Olorin*."

Keyshia thanked the priest, and Poju drove them, lost in thought, back to her office.

CHAPTER 15

THE THIEF

Over tea, the women strategized.

“Ayotunde, I have wrestled with this for several months. I feel like I’m in an Agatha Christie novel, but I’m not a detective like Miss Marple.”

“Keyshia, is Olorin a Yoruba surname?”

“Not ordinarily. It means ‘artist.’”

They fell silent again, then Keyshia snapped her fingers and pointed across her desk.

“Ayotunde, in that file cabinet is the contact list for Madame Wenger’s mentorship program. She brings young artists to the grove to study. There may be a clue there.”

“Keyshia, you’re becoming more like Miss Marple by the minute!”

They scanned the list. The first column was typed surnames, the second column first names, followed by home addresses in Osogbo. Halfway down the list was a blank first column. In the second column was a single word: Olorin.

"Ayotunde, have Poju bring the car around."

Poju drove them to a working-class neighborhood. Children crowded the streets. The little girls played tinko-tinko, clapping intricate patterns at high speed, while the teenaged boys practiced *dambe* boxing. The VW turned down a quiet street, and Poju found the house. It was a stucco cottage with a tin-roofed shed in the back. A goat and a few chickens wandered in the yard. Keyshia knocked on the door. A middle-aged woman answered, looking worried. Keyshia greeted her.

"*Se o nso* English?"

The woman shook her head. Keyshia raised her voice.

"Anyone in this household *se o nso* English?"

The woman shook her head again and made a sweeping motion for them to leave. Then a voice called from the back of the house.

"*Iya*, it's okay."

A teenaged girl came forward and hugged her mother.

"It's okay. I know why they are here."

She beckoned the two visitors to follow her through the house into the backyard. At the door of the tin shed, she turned.

"I'm sorry."

She opened the door and they entered. The afternoon sun slanted through open seams in the corrugated roof, illuminating a workshop, and a gallery of terra-cotta masks. Each one was of master quality, and each one represented a goddess. Near the kiln was a half-finished mask of Yemoja, the mother of all things, and on an iron stand was the mask from the sacred grove of Osun. Ayotunde and Keyshia looked at each other, incredulously. The girl spoke first.

"I'm sorry, truly sorry. I live here with my mother. With no father in the house, there is no income. I have no money to attend the academy in Benin. My dream is to honor *ifa* with my art, and to someday take these images out of Nigeria and show them to the world. I am just a poor girl, but I am rich in dreams."

Ayotunde gestured around the shed. "Not only in dreams, but in talent as well, I would say! So you have borrowed masks from the grove and learned from them, because you have no money to study and apprentice with an art teacher, then you return the originals to the grove?"

Olorin smiled apologetically. "Perhaps I am a criminal."

"I get the sense that you are more of a dedicated artist than a thief. Artists will sometimes go to extremes to nurture their inspiration. Does your mother know about this?"

"She knows I am working on art, but she doesn't know about the pieces from the grove."

Ayotunde's face was serious. "Olorin, art thieves live in a world of bad people, even if they start with good intentions. I don't want you going down that path. Listen to me."

She took Olorin's hands in hers.

"There was a man in New York by the name of Alistair Wulver. A wealthy man. When he went to *orun-rere*, the spirit world, he left a considerable fortune for the purpose of giving educational opportunities to talented young women. I can look around this room and see that you fit that description. If your mother agrees, I will send for you to come to America next month, where your talent can blossom. You will find buyers for your work there, and you can send money back to support your mother."

Olorin nodded enthusiastically.

"My mother will agree, no worries!"

"Fine. I return to New York tomorrow, and I will set things up. Miss Ojo will contact you from the museum with the timetable and travel arrangements. All I ask is that you allow her to return Yemoja to her place in the grove, for the benefit of all the pilgrims."

"Yes, yes, and thank you, thank you!"
The shed was now all smiles.

CHAPTER 16

THE COUP

The following morning, July 29, Poju pulled up at the departures gate at Lagos airport. He pulled the front trunk release handle, and Ayotunde grabbed her duffel bag. There was another parcel in the luggage compartment, wrapped in brown paper.

"Miss Ojo from the grove wanted you to have this. It's your *orisha*, your protector spirit."

Poju smiled warmly as Ayotunde unwrapped a small terracotta mask.

"It's Osun, to whom the grove is dedicated."

Ayotunde did a double take. Then she smiled. The mask was the face of Abeni, the face she first saw on the flight from London, the woman who mentored her on her first day in Yorubaland.

"Thank you for everything, Poju."

As she shook his hand, they heard an explosion coming from the direction of the marina. Poju's warm smile turned to stone.

"That's the statehouse! The coup is beginning. Tunde *run*, don't walk, to your gate. Show your Strabo credentials, and immigration might let you through. Your plane to London may still take off before the airport shuts down."

"What about you, Poju?"

Gunfire could now be heard in the direction of the statehouse.

"I'm driving straight north, back to Ile-Ife. I need to be on campus for whatever happens next. Now go, go!"

Inside the terminal, chaos was erupting. Ayotunde pushed her way through panicked crowds all heading in the opposite direction, toward the exits. She was breathless when she reached the BOAC desk. She laid her passport on the counter. The perforated remainder of her roundtrip ticket served as her confirmation and boarding pass. She struggled to appear confident, but her voice was shaking.

"Flight 880 to London, through Rome and connecting at Heathrow with TWA flight 777 to New York."

The attendant perused her papers thoughtfully, then shook his head.

"I'm sorry, madam. That flight is boarding no further passengers. You can see we are in an emergency. It will be departing as soon as the ground crew has completed fueling."

"No! You don't understand! I'm sorry, I…I…oh, there is this."

She produced her Strabo Society identification card. Now her hands were shaking as well. The attendant read it and picked up his walkie talkie. He spoke softly in Hausa. Ayotunde bit her lip, regretting that she knew a few words in Yoruba but none in Hausa. She anxiously took note of the fact that he was deliberately not using English. He clicked the radio off and turned to her.

"Please wait right here, madam. You are not to leave the airport."

It suddenly occurred to her that, at the onset of a revolution, she had no idea which side the airport staff might be on, and no idea on which side her affiliation with Strabo would place her.

Was she being detained? A political prisoner? A hostage? She had a sudden impulse to run, but the attendant had her papers and besides, where would she go? There was nowhere safe in Lagos, and within minutes there would be no way to get back home to the States. Her only chance was to wait.

A second man, in a security guard uniform with a holstered gun, arrived and closely examined the card. The two men continued speaking in Hausa, with occasional words in English. The second man, older and glancing around nervously, gestured toward Ayotunde.

"American?"

The younger man nodded.

The older man leaned in closer, speaking softly in Hausa, but Ayotunde picked out the English words.

"CIA...NSA..."

After several minutes of whispering, nodding and pointing at their subject, the older man departed and the younger man returned to the counter. He handed Ayotunde her passport, boarding pass, and Strabo credentials.

"Fueling will be finished in five minutes and the hatchway will then be locked. You are cleared if you can make it to Gate 15A in time."

Ayotunde broke every record she had set on the women's track team at Scarsdale High to reach the gate. An attendant held the terminal door open and whispered *"Arire daada"* as she rushed past. The Yoruba wish for good luck worked. She raced across the tarmac and up the gangway. A British stewardess waved her on board, then gestured to the ground crew. The hatchway closed behind Ayotunde as she plopped into the first vacant seat. The VC-10 was already beginning to taxi down the runway as she fastened her seat belt. While the plane picked up speed, Ayotunde could see smoke rising from the Lagos city center.

As the aircraft lifted into the air and banked north, Ayotunde opened her backpack and whispered "thanks" to the little mask of Osun, her protector spirit. She suddenly felt sleepy as the last of her adrenaline drained away. She could nap until the layover in Rome, and then it was on to London, where she would connect with her TWA return flight home. As she drifted off to sleep, a comforting thought came to her, and she whispered to the little Yoruba mask she was still clutching on her lap.

"Hmm…I wonder if Artemis is lounging by the sea in Italy at this very moment?"

PART THREE

The Lycanthrope

CHAPTER 17

A CHANGE IN PLANS

The waves lapping on the beaches of Sardinia looked lovely, even from ten thousand feet, as Artemis's Alitalia flight descended toward Rome. She rechecked her itinerary.

Disembark airport Flumicino, no checked bags. Diplomatic visa. Train to Rome Termini station, transfer train to Napoli Centrale station, to be met in Plazza Garibaldi by driver bearing Strabo signage for transport to Castel Nuovo.

She glanced over her notes for the lecture. "The Lycanthrope of Ravello" was an old Italian story, issuing from that misty region of legend that lurks between fable and fact. The hilltop village of Ravello, the historic summer home of popes and a sun-drenched hideaway for artists, writers, and actors, has in its history periodically succumbed to panic over rumors of a werewolf stalking the narrow streets and lemon gardens under the full moon.

Artemis's published article about her were-wolverine encounter had gained her some notoriety as a scholar on the subject, and on occasion a lecture engagement could serve as cover for an intelligence mission. She wondered if Strabo had more in mind for her than a simple speech on this trip.

The sun was high over Naples Bay as Artemis walked out onto the plaza, looking for a friendly cab driver with the Strabo sign. She spotted the sign, but instead of a casually clad cabbie, it was held by an anxious-looking cleric. He was dressed in a brown woolen robe, a three-knotted cincture around his waist, and sandals on his feet. He greeted her in two languages.

"*Ciao,* Signorina Fletcher." And then, in English, "We must go quickly."

He carried her duffel bag to a battered Lancia Appia, and spoke again in English.

"It's not a limo, but it will get us there…the Franciscan vow of poverty, you know."

She settled in the passenger seat.

"How far is the castle?"

He veered through the chaotic plaza traffic, sidestepping her question.

"*Primo*, let me apologize for my haste, and my negligence in failing to properly introduce myself. I am Brother Faunus, and as you have no doubt guessed, I am a Franciscan. Not a priest, but a lay brother."

He narrowly avoided a rear-end collision by skirting around a tiny Vespa truck, which took them briefly onto the sidewalk and then back on the road. Instead of continuing on Corso Umberto 1 toward the castle, he turned south, heading along the bay, toward Mount Vesuvius, Pompeii, and the Amalfi peninsula.

"I'd like to get across the Monti Lattari before dark. The Amalfi roads were meant for slow-moving donkeys in the Middle Ages, not modern autos careening around switchbacks."

His American accent was unmistakable.

"So, Brother Faunus, I gather that there has been a change of plans, and I'm not heading for the Castel Nuovo after all."

"Signorina Fletcher..."

"Please just call me Artemis, and maybe explain your Bronx accent."

"Of course. I will clarify how I came to the Amalfi Coast from New York, and I will tell you why Kevin Macduff has sent you here on behalf of Strabo."

"I'm guessing there is no speech, correct?"

"Your expertise is needed elsewhere. There is a crisis."

Artemis was used to being kept in the dark about the purpose of a mission until she met with her contact. She smiled and raised an eyebrow.

"I suppose the crisis doesn't involve the Lycanthrope of Ravello."

He glanced over at her, then turned back to negotiate the upward-winding road.

"As a matter of fact, it does."

CHAPTER 18

THE CHAPEL

After they passed the exits for Vesuvius and Pompeii, Brother Faunus fell silent, turning his attention to the road as they crossed over the agricultural district on the high ridge, where lemon groves clung to steep hillsides. Tortuous switchbacks traversed cliffs that plunged into deep ravines, and a truck or bus coming the other way on the narrow road required careful detente on the part of both drivers. They crossed the ridge summit of Monti Lattari, and for the first time, the Gulf of Salerno came into view. The Lancia pulled up at a small, whitewashed chapel perched on a cliff overlooking the seacoast below.

"This is the Sanctuary of Santa Maria del Bando. I was assigned here after my studies at the American College in Rome. Not being an ordained priest, I don't say the Mass, but I perform services of various types for the parishioners in the area. That includes the village of Atrani below, and Ravello above, as well as sometimes getting an assignment from the Cattedrale di Sant'Andrea down in Amalfi."

He opened the unlocked door, and they entered the tiny chapel. Votive candles illuminated artworks and cast shadows on the stucco walls. Frankincense permeated the air. Artemis felt a wave of peace emanating from a Renaissance-era painting of the Madonna above the altar. She momentarily thought she heard a voice, a déjà vu, perhaps, of her visit to a temple in Katmandu. She recovered quickly and wrote it off as travel fatigue. Brother Faunus broke the silence.

"The services I perform are not the kind I might be doing back in New York. The people here—and I mean the farmers in the hills, not the tourists—share a trove of beliefs that stretch back further than Christianity, to Rome and further back beyond the Etruscans and the Greeks. We have no way of knowing their origin. My task as a cleric is to accommodate those beliefs, things that many would call superstitions, while caring for their souls according to my Franciscan training."

"Brother Faunus, I've learned that superstitions are often mysteries that science and academia have been unable to solve. Most of them have a deep connection to nature, so they've gone unexplored in our era, when humanity sees itself as conquering the earth, rather than harmonizing with it."

He nodded in agreement as they returned to the car.

"I'll give you an example, Artemis. Yesterday I was called to a lemon grove up on the terraced slopes. A stranger had been seen looking at the trees, and there was fear that the evil eye might have been laid on them. There is actually an ancient blessing to dispel the evil eye, and I administered it."

He glanced at her. She sensed that he was checking for a sign of skepticism. She sought to reassure him that she began every mission with a tabula rasa, her mind a blank sheet of paper, ready to be written upon by events and circumstances.

"Brother Faunus, I was raised without religion. I suppose the crossbow was my religion, but as a student of the Middle Ages, I've been immersed in Christian history as an outsider. In your case, as a follower of St. Francis, I suppose you are part of a nature-centered community, maybe even one that blends the old pagan beliefs with orthodoxy."

"Artemis, I'm glad to hear that you don't scoff at these things. I will drive you down to your lodging in Amalfi and explain how I got here along the way."

CHAPTER 19

EPIPHANY

Brother Faunus turned on the headlights as they negotiated the downhill curves.

"As you guessed, I was born and raised in New York City. Arthur Avenue in the Bronx, to be exact. You remember the vocal group Dion and the Belmonts?"

"The only music I'm familiar with is the thirteenth-century French troubadours, so I have to plead ignorance."

"Well, Dion DiMucci was a neighbor of mine, from Belmont Avenue, the next block over. It's an Italian neighborhood. My grandparents spoke Italian, and I grew up with two languages. I attended Catholic school, of course, but I spent most of my time at the Bronx Zoo, a short walk from home. Animals fascinated me, and I felt a sort of identification with them, a kinship. I spent my freshman year down the street at Fordham. I wanted to study philology, the sources and meaning of words, but when I read a book titled *Riprap* by a poet named Gary Snyder, I felt like I had found a kindred spirit, and I discovered the Beat movement. Are you familiar with it?"

"Once again, Brother Faunus, poetry to me means Dante and Chaucer."

"Well, I dropped out of college and headed straight for Greenwich Village. I lived the Beat lifestyle. Late nights in jazz clubs, part of a cohort of rebels trying to push the limits of literature, even the limits of culture. It was probably the opposite in every way from your disciplined upbringing. That's why you became a professor, while I was basically a dropout."

Artemis took a glance at the sea below them. The sun was getting low, and the gulf was turning pied shades of luminous green.

"But both of our paths led us here, didn't they?"

"Mine was a winding one. Even living in Greenwich Village, I never lost my love for nature, and I would escape to the Adirondacks to bring me back to myself, so to speak. It was on one of those trips that it happened."

Artemis didn't ask what "it" was. She knew he would continue.

"It was two years ago, in mid-April. The ice was melting on the lakes and rivers, and I was taking a solo canoe trip, just me and my backpack, on the Raquette River up near Tupper Lake, in the heart of the Adirondacks. The weather had been clear, and the sun was going down. I was looking for a spot to tie up for the night and camp when a squall came up out of nowhere. The Raquette is usually calm, but it turned into a torrent. It all happened so fast that my canoe swamped and I went under. The current carried the canoe away, and my backpack sank like a stone—too many books, I guess. I got a lungful of water and everything went dark. I can't tell you what happened next, because I don't know. I do know that I don't remember swimming to shore, but I woke up in daylight on the bank. I recognized the place. It's called the crusher. There used to be a machine there that pulverized rock into gravel. I always took it as a metaphor for grinding raw stone into something of value. Maybe that's what happened to me."

He came to a stop while a flock of sheep crossed the road in the gathering shadows.

"Artemis, I had what we call an epiphany. Sort of a revelation. For me, it was a vocation. That comes from the Latin *voce*, voice. I heard it. I was lying on the bank gathering my strength to try to stand up, and I heard a voice as clearly as I can hear your voice now."

"Did you recognize it, like recalling a friend or a relative? Maybe part of recovering from nearly drowning?"

"This might sound crazy, but I'm not sure that I 'nearly' drowned. Do you remember the line from *The Tempest* where the character suffered a sea change? I think that happened to me."

"I don't think that's crazy. What did the voice say?"

"This is why I'm here, and why I'm wearing this wool robe and sandals. The voice was singing the 'Canticle of the Sun.' Do you know it?"

"Of course. I'm a professor! Before he was Saint Francis, Giovanni di Pietro di Bernardone wrote that, one of the great medieval poems. Finally, something that falls into my area of expertise!"

"Well, that's what the voice was singing to me when I woke up on the riverbank, in that dense forest. If you recall, it's a Christian hymn of praise, but it can also be read as an ode to the older pagan beliefs, invoking the nature manifestations of the gods: the sun, the moon, wind, water, fire, and earth. It's unlike any other Christian hymn, and it seemed to call me. That was the vocation. There is an ancient belief that one hears a voice that sets them on a spirit quest. In my case, it led me to hitch a ride back to the city, where I went directly to the Franciscan monastery near Washington Square. They saw something in me, the gravel ground out of rock at the crusher, and they packed me off to the American College in Rome. It was there that I took the name Brother Faunus, a brother to nature, from the old Etruscan god. From there I was sent here to the peninsula to serve the people."

"This epiphany, as you call it, happened in the Adirondacks, two years ago?"

"That's right. I feel like my old directionless life ended on that river, and this one was somehow granted to me. A sea change."

As the last of the flock of sheep crossed the road, he turned to Artemis as if to punctuate his story and confirm his sincerity. For the first time, she looked directly into his eyes, and her own eyes widened with the shock of recognition. She felt like she knew them.

CHAPTER 20

MOONRISE

As the sun settled lower, they walked across the plaza in front of the cathedral of Saint Andrew in Amalfi.

"Your room is ready for you at the Hotel Croce. You walk up seventy-five steps to get there. You'll find that there are always steps in Amalfi! I will meet you here at the cathedral plaza in the morning. You recall that I said there is a local crisis. I will explain fully, but now there is no time. *Buona notte*, Artemis."

Artemis hiked up the seventy-five steps and checked into her room, a spacious Moorish-style chamber with glazed tile walls arrayed in arabesques that recalled the ancient days when Amalfi was a tiny independent republic. She dropped her duffel bag inside the door and climbed another staircase to a rooftop patio looking out over the gulf. The calm sea was bathed in emerald light, as the full moon rose.

CHAPTER 21

THE SONG

Artemis woke with a start. She clicked her wristwatch. Two a.m. Something other than jet lag had roused her. A robe hung by the bed. She pulled it on, opened the door, and crept up the stone stairs to the rooftop. She heard it again. A lonesome, otherworldly sound. No one would call it a howl. Somewhere above Amalfi, on the steep slopes of the Monti Lattari, a wolf was singing his song of praise to Sister Moon.

CHAPTER 22

ESPRESSO

In the morning, Brother Faunus was sitting on the steps of the Duomo. The massive black and white Arab-style facade behind him was a "recent" addition, in the 1800s, to the thirteenth-century cathedral, and the towering belfry had been a landmark for sailors since the original construction replaced an earlier Roman temple. The cathedral faced away from Europe, looking across the sea toward Africa and Asia Minor, a perfect symbol of the exoticism of Amalfi. Brother Faunus stood and waved to Artemis as she completed her downhill hike from the hotel.

"Artemis, *buongiorno*!" He motioned to an outdoor table and called out. *"Due caffè, per favore."* The waiter bowed.

"Certo."

They made themselves comfortable.

"So, how are the accommodations?"

"Lovely. Like being cosseted in the chambers of a Byzantine empress."

"Spoken like a true medieval scholar! How did you sleep?"

Something about the question triggered Artemis's close-to-the-vest reflex.

"Fine, Brother. Thank you for making the arrangements."

She felt that there was a kindred spirit somewhere within the coarse wool vestments, but it was a wary spirit, hiding something. The two espressos arrived, and they stirred, she looking at the sea, and he looking back at the Duomo.

"Brother Faunus, you told me when you spirited me away to this idyllic spot that there was a crisis. I seem to recall you promising to enlighten me in the morning. So far I've learned more about the Bronx than I have about Amalfi. I know Macduff only detours me for a reason, and you're the one who can elucidate it."

Brother Faunus sighed.

"Of course. Allow me to begin with a story. It's an old one, but it will illuminate the present situation."

He took his first sip and drew a playing card from under his tunic.

CHAPTER 23

THE CARD

Brother Faunus lay the card on the table. It was not part of a suit—not hearts, spades, clubs, or diamonds. Instead there was a term printed across the bottom in Gothic script: *Forza d'Animo*. The rest of the card's face was a picture of a mountainous countryside like Amalfi. Two figures occupied the foreground. The first was a woman dressed in medieval peasant garb, but with a crown of vegetation. Her gown was cinched with a garland of red roses. The second figure was a magnificently maned male lion. Strangely, the lion's flanks were pressed against the lady's legs, like an affectionate dog. Even more strangely, the lady was effortlessly holding the lion's jaws open with her bare hands. Above her head, like a halo, floated the leminscate, the traditional figure eight sign of infinity. Her face was impassive, peaceful. Artemis scanned the card, considering each image.

"It's a tarot card. I've seen a more modern version, where the word at the bottom is *strength*."

"That would be Pamela Colman Smith's artwork. Pixie Smith, she was called. Studied art at Pratt in New York, and later befriended Yeats in London."

"Yeats. Just last week I was fighting an Irish wizard with his sword."

"Artemis, if anyone else had told me that..." He trailed off. "But in your case there's almost nothing I wouldn't believe."

She shrugged, and he went on.

"The Italian term translates as 'strength of spirit.' A bit different from just 'strength,' wouldn't you say?"

"No one from Pratt made the woodcut that this card was printed from. It's old."

"Very old. The full deck has been in the possession of the cathedral here since the Knights Templar left it, along with what they claimed to be the bones of St. Andrew, after the collapse of the Crusades at the end of the thirteenth century. The Crypt of St. Andrew is right behind us."

He took his last sip.

"The tarot deck had four suits, the origin of our modern suits, but it had an additional twenty-two cards called 'the major arcana.' These were heavily symbolic pictographs that could be read as a sort of book, dealing with philosophy, psychology, and spirituality."

"So were they Christian icons?"

"Not officially. Since they mixed Christian doctrine with earlier, nature-centered beliefs, they didn't meet the rigors of orthodoxy, so they were hidden from the inquisitors in plain sight as a card game for the cognoscenti, or a fortune-telling gimmick. If you look at each image, though, they are a compendium of ancient insights."

"By nature-centered you mean pagan?"

"Pagan is derived from *paisan*, a country person, or a hillbilly in America. It was used by the early Christians to deride folks outside the urban centers who preferred the old beliefs."

"Spoken like a true philologist."

"Touché! So, Artemis, what do you see at first glance?"

"The woman has the physical strength to subdue a lion, and the courage to actually do it. She could be an actual person, like Joan of Arc."

"Ah, but we know that Joan of Arc really lived and died. That's in history books, and when we see a picture of her, we know who it is."

"Well, my studies tell me that medieval storytelling was always allegorical. Every image, and every character, represented something else. Something bigger."

"Yes, yes."

The card lay on the table, between the two demitasse cups. Artemis studied it.

"She could represent both strength and courage, as an encouragement to others to be strong and brave."

"Of course, and she does. Dig a little deeper, though, and consider the original title, 'strength of spirit.' Are there any weapons in the picture?"

"No, but there are plenty of roses."

"An alchemical symbol. Yeats used it frequently, and alchemy is itself an allegorical symbol. On the surface, it seems to be about chemistry, changing base material into gold. Of course, in times past that would be the ultimate magic, but the symbol points to an even higher magic, and it's revealed in the image of the woman subduing the lion without weapons."

Artemis took her own last sip.

"Go on."

"The lion is the base material, that is to say, the human's lower self. Uncontrolled destructive impulses, the Christian seven deadly sins, or the Buddhist idea of desire as the source of all suffering. The lion's goal is to be the king of beasts. That drive is the source of war, slavery, genocide. We've seen it play out in our own century. Now, the character on the card? Her subjugation of that lower self is the alchemical gold, depicted on the card as victory over the lion. I believe that is the allegorical story told here. It is an encouragement, but to an even higher goal than just being strong and brave. It's achieving an inner power of the spirit. *Forza d'animo*."

Brother Faunus's relentlessly logical analysis was like an injection of adrenaline to Artemis, but she used her undercover-agent poker face to hide her excitement. She wanted to see the other twenty-one major arcana cards right away, but they were locked in a vault, and she had to stay focused on her mission.

"So the face of this card is like a book of philosophy that could be understood by illiterate persons, which I suppose was almost everyone in Europe in the Middle Ages. This is tremendously enlightening, but is it all leading up to telling me what the local crisis is?"

"Yes, but first, one more story. It's a lovely, sunny day. Would you care to take a hike?"

CHAPTER 24

THE MOUNTAIN OF THREE HILLS

Brother Faunus urged the Lancia up harrowing switchbacks to a small village of Bomerano in the Agerola district. He parked next to the central square water pump.

"We'll talk while we walk."

He slung his backpack over his shoulder. Undeterred by his clerical garb of wool robe and sandals, he set out toward the west. Two blocks from the square, the settlement came to an abrupt end. The only structure was a cracked concrete stairway that led up a seemingly endless mountain.

"Even during the millennia when temples and churches were the only buildings over two stories, the ancients kept themselves busy building stairways, straight up mountains! This is called the mountain of three hills."

In the absence of any other trekkers, the steep route was deserted. They climbed the stairway single file, settling into the kind of synchronicity that develops among hikers on the trail. Faunus knew the trail and led the way, keeping up a running narration that toggled between enlightening and evasive. His tendency to be both brilliant and cryptic was frustrating, but it kept her interest piqued. She decided to just let him talk. The walk was relaxing him, but whatever he was hiding, she sensed that she couldn't draw it out by cajoling him. Either it was something he felt the need to break to her gradually, or perhaps it was something he had to admit to himself gradually. They came to a rocky outcrop where they stopped to catch their breath. There was a signpost in Italian, French, and English.

Caution. Wild pigs are present.

Faunus furrowed his brow.

"We need to take that seriously, Artemis. I may be an animal lover, but those creatures are dangerous."

"Perhaps I could subdue one without weapons."

He smiled.

"That all depends on your strength of spirit, doesn't it? Hey, you never know. You might get your chance up in these hills."

Near the summit, the trail disappeared and they scrambled over boulders, catching their breath at the top. The view was transporting. The red roofs of Amalfi lay far below them to the east, the bustle of Positano to the west. The emerald gulf, dotted with white sails, stretched before them to the horizon. Brother Faunus produced a small clay-fired bottle of Piedirosso, two wineglasses, a loaf of bread, and a block of Parmigiano-Reggiano wrapped in paper. They sat on a flat boulder and basked in the Amalfi sunlight.

They ate silently for a while, absorbing the towering natural surroundings. An occasional small cloud drifted below them. Brother Faunus broke the silence.

"My patron, Saint Francis, is revered as an example of humility and simplicity, but in some ways he was a complicated man. Giovanni di Pietro di Bernardone grew up in a wealthy household. His father was a rich merchant, and his mother was from an aristocratic family in the south of France. His lifestyle was probably something like mine in Greenwich Village. Once he had his epiphany he was a saintly Christian, but he also embodied the ancient worship of nature. He could be Bacchus, Pan, Orpheus..."

"Or Faunus, the old Etruscan forest god."

"Or Faunus indeed. His 'Canticle of the Sun' is one of the most beautiful Christian hymns precisely because it seems to predate Christianity. It reaches back to a world that we can never fully know from written history. We have only the utterances of mystics like Francis, passed down through ages before him, to get a sense of that life, truly immersed in nature, not struggling to conquer it. That, to him, was the higher self, and because it was beyond desire, it had the outward appearance of humility and simplicity. He was wealthy for sure, but in a richer way."

"I can see why you identify so strongly with him, but how does his story tie in with the tarot card?"

"In thirteenth-century Umbria, near Assisi, where Francis lived and established his monastery, there was, and still is, a walled town called Gubbio, on the slope of Mount Ingino. The residents reported hearing the howling of a wolf under the full moon, and the stories grew to include sightings of a vicious beast that threatened the sheep and goats. The terrified townspeople appealed to Francis, who was known for his kinship with animals. According to the story, he ventured out of the town gates and met the wolf under the full moon. The animal recognized him as a brother, and Francis embraced him. On some level, they communicated, and a deal was struck whereby the wolf would guarantee the safety of the local livestock in exchange for simple food, provided by the townsfolk, that would otherwise go to waste. It could be said that to ensure the pact, both the wolf and the people would have to rise above their lower selves, and their hatred born of prejudice, or prejudgment. Francis was the negotiator. Do you see where I'm going with this?"

"I not only see, I think I'm a couple of steps ahead of you. If the story is read as an allegory, the wolf is Giovanni di Pietro de Benardone's lower self, which has kept him within the walls of his lifestyle, until he tames the wolf, makes peace with it, and rises to the freedom of his higher self, Saint Francis."

"As the woman does in the tarot card."

"As in the tarot card."

They stumbled down a slope of rocky scree to reach a narrow, deserted road leading back to the town square. Their only company was a mule, who brayed loudly at them from his stable door as they passed.

CHAPTER 25

THE REVELATION

The Lancia pulled up in front of Saint Andrew's Square in Amalfi. Across the boulevard, tourists were disembarking from the ferry boats returning from Capri. The shadows were growing long. Brother Faunus left the engine running, shifted into neutral, and yanked up the parking brake. Artemis reached for the door handle, but she had one more question.

"So the story is an allegory, perhaps even an alchemical tale. The man overcomes his lower self, represented by the wolf, and is transfigured, undergoes a sea change into his higher self, a saint. Does that mean the legends surrounding Ravello, just up the ridge from us, are allegorical as well, or are they superstition on the part of the local farmers?"

He drummed his fingers on the steering wheel for a full thirty seconds.

"Artemis, you've been asking me all day for a clue as to your mission here. In fact, you had the clue in your possession when you landed in Rome. The invitation was to speak about the wolfman, the Lycanthrope of Ravello, correct?"

"Correct. The legend, or perhaps an ancient allegory."

"It was neither."

He turned to face her, and once again she recognized the eyes, the yellowish tint when the moon was full. She silently warned herself not to recoil when he leaned in and whispered.

"Artemis, the wolf is back."

CHAPTER 26

THE MOTORCYCLE

She twisted the door handle and got out of the car, shaken. Faunus shouted over the traffic noise.

"Meet me at the chapel just after sunrise!"

He threw the four-speed shifter into gear, pulled out onto the boulevard, and made a perilous U-turn, heading east toward Atrani and, from there, the winding road up to the chapel. Artemis stood still for a moment, taking deep breaths, slowing her pulse to where she could think clearly. She felt alternating waves of terror and pity, but it was too much to sort out now. There was no time. The moon was on the rise. She climbed the steps to the Hotel Croce. Before going to her room, she stopped at the concierge desk.

"I need to rent a motorcycle."

"Of course, madam. I will make the arrangements. When do you need it?"

"Now." She flashed her Strabo identification.

"*Certamente.* It will be waiting for you at the bottom of the steps in thirty minutes."

She tossed a flashlight and a pair of leather gloves into her backpack and laced her boots. At eight p.m. she was gunning a Ducati Sport up the Via Santo Sebastian.

CHAPTER 27

THE HUNT

The Santuario Santa Maria del Bando was empty. Votive candles were lit on the altar, beneath the painting of the Virgin. From the high rocky outcropping, the gulf shimmered like an emerald grotto under the full moon. Artemis crinkled her nose as an offshore breeze swept the cliffside. A pungent odor permeated the air, doing battle with the fragrance of the lemon groves. The wolf had marked his den. The ground was too dry to reveal tracks, and a wild animal would be unlikely to leave any obvious visual evidence of its path through the underbrush.

Then she heard it. Halfway up the mountain, the wolf was singing in his high lonesome sound. She kick-started the motorbike. The Ducati could hit eighty miles per hour if she pushed it, but she wouldn't be able to maintain that when she hit the switchbacks on the Strada di Ravello. By the time she reached the village, the streets were empty and silent. She parked the bike and walked, scanning the garden walls of the Villa Rufolo with her flashlight and listening for any sound that might betray the animal's location. It came almost on cue, but it was distant, down the ridge and off to the west.

Artemis opened the throttle, and when she hit the first downhill switchback, she jumped the bike off the road and followed her headlight beam down the bumpy slope and through the terraced lemon groves. Going off-road was only slightly less dangerous than the mountain *strada*. The howling continued. He was heading toward a steep ravine where the River Schiato met the gulf. She would need a road to negotiate the terrain. She turned west, downhill toward the ravine on the Via Maggio. The road took a sharp curve where a footpath made the final descent to a shallow ford in the river. She jumped the Ducati off-road again and headed full speed down the dirt path. As she met the cool air in the deep canyon, she heard the sound of *campanelli*, little bells. A flock of goats were slowly crossing the ford, taking time to play king of the mountain on the river boulders. They ignored the human on her idling motorbike, making it clear that she was on their turf and their schedule. Artemis heard the wolf again. He was on the other side of the river, heading up the west side of the canyon, toward Agerola on the high ridge. With no clue to the water depth on either side of the ford, there was nothing she could do but wait for the goats to move on.

Minutes seemed like hours while she waited, and when she was finally able to get across, the wolf cries were distant, up the mountain. She decided to take the Ducati straight up the steep footpath. With no nighttime pedestrian traffic, she was able to maintain speed as her headlight pushed up the narrow trail. Climbing higher, the moonlight revealed a tiny structure high on the near-vertical slope. She cut her engine and parked the bike. Her flashlight found a narrow, steep trail. The building, if it could be called that, was just big enough for one occupant. An oak chair, built like a church pew with a kneeler, and a small desk were the only furnishings. It looked to be centuries old. Artemis took note of all of that, but it was the scent of the wolf's territorial marking that she noticed first.

The wolf howled again, closer this time but farther up the mountain, toward the village of Bomerano, the same trailhead where she had hiked with Faunus earlier that day. She kick-started the cycle and continued up the trail, slowly this time, listening to the sounds of the night. As the path turned north, leading up to the still-distant town square, the moonlight illuminated a deep ravine leading down to the gulf, far below her. Across the chasm more lemon groves clung to the cliffs in steep terraces.

The wolf howled, this time very close to her. Was he leading her somewhere? She had been on an adrenaline-fueled vector since sundown, and now in the dead of night, she took a moment to consider what she would actually do if she met the creature at this lonely spot. She had no weapon, nor did she have any commission to injure the wolf. She recalled the tarot card and the story of the wolf of Gubbio, and how carefully worded Brother Faunus's seemingly rambling narrative had been. He was *instructing* her on how to deal with this moment. As a special agent, she was normally a woman of action. Her crossbow was her partner, but she had no crossbow on the mountain. Faunus had trained her in a kind of diplomacy with nature, a way to achieve rapprochement with an animal. Before she could accomplish that, though, she would have to survive her own encounter with the beast. It was a lot to consider, but there was no time for consideration.

The wolf howled again, a muted wail that seemed to come from within the mountain itself. She parked the bike and walked slowly along the path, not looking down at the sheer drop to the valley. Her flashlight revealed an opening. A cave. Then another one. There were half a dozen openings, each one the size of a door, in the rocky mountainside. As she approached, she saw designs etched in the rock face. She recognized them as medieval Christian icons, Latin phrases carved out in the shape of the crucifix, a fish, and other symbols. Immediately she realized this place and the lonely hut further down the cliff were once the abode of monks, hermits who spent months or even years in solitude, absorbed in prayer. Their intense piety made the total isolation bearable. That was centuries ago, and the hut and caves, carved from stone, stood like lonely reminders of a bygone era of deep mystical faith. Whether the wolf was conscious of that, whether he was seeking shelter or just evading the sound of the approaching motorcycle, was not for Artemis to know. What she did know is that she had to enter the cave complex.

As she shone her light on the first entrance, the one farthest south on the trail, she thought back to her initial encounter with Alistair Wulver. Under the full moon, he was the wolverine charging toward her atop the Kensico Dam, and she was the hunter bringing the crossbow to her shoulder. That night, instead of attacking, he saved her life. Her vulnerability had somehow awakened the compassionate nature of Wulver the man, his strength of spirit. If she met up with the wolf inside the cave, would that scenario play out again? If not, she was completely defenseless. She pictured the tarot card again. *Forza d'animo.* She gathered her own strength of spirit and stepped into the cave.

CHAPTER 28

THE WOLF'S DEN

The den-marking smell permeated the first chamber, but there was no wolf. Passageways, natural formations created over centuries by limestone erosion, linked the half-dozen caves in the complex. As she moved from one to the next, she knew that if the wolf was still in one of them, he would be aware of her scent and the sound of her footsteps before she ever spotted him. That would mean he would either be gone or be waiting for her. A veteran hunter, she didn't like surrendering that much control to her quarry.

She moved slowly from chamber to chamber. The musky canine odor grew stronger as the trail became fresher. She took a deep breath and centered herself before entering the last chamber. It was empty, but her sixth sense, the one that integrated and interpreted the other five senses, told her that the occupant had departed just before she entered. She could feel a lingering energy, a presence. It was an aura of strangeness that had radiated around Wulver, and now she detected it again. It was more than a territorial marker. It was a message, a summons. At once all of her anxiety vanished. She saw clearly where she was to go next, and what she was to do there.

Outside, the wolf cried again, down the footpath, heading back down toward the ravine. Artemis rode the other way, up the mountain into the deserted Bomerano town square. She took the ridge-top highway east and opened up the throttle.

CHAPTER 29

WELL MET BY MOONLIGHT

The chapel was deserted when she arrived. Brother Faunus had told her to meet him just after sunrise. She arrived just *before* sunrise. The votive candles had burned out. The eastern glow was just beginning to creep through the windows. In the murky light, with a mist of frankincense still hanging in the air, Artemis sat on a velvet-cushioned chair in the tiny sanctuary. She began to feel the effects of a night without sleep. Her eyelids half closed, she thought she saw the eyes of the Virgin above the altar turn in her direction. She heard a voice whisper, *"Forza d'animo."* Her eyes opened suddenly. She bolted awake.

The wolf was at the door. He stood still, growled, then advanced slowly toward Artemis, his tail held high. Halfway down the aisle he stopped and bared his teeth. The fangs were long and sharp, quite unlike those of a domesticated dog. A wild animal's weapon. With no weapon of her own, Artemis could only stay still and wait. The beast advanced, stopping again to sniff the air, never taking its eyes off of the invader in his den.

Artemis stood up, and the creature shied away for a moment, then advanced again. This time its tail was lowered. The wolf crouched before her, pawing the floor. She motioned for it to stand. With its tail still lowered, it pressed against her leg and looked up at her. She knew the eyes, and she knew where she had seen them before. She felt no fear, only intense pity. She glanced up again at the painting of the Virgin, the Earth Mother, and then she gently took the wolf's upper and lower jaws, one in each hand, and opened them, bending over him in an attitude of compassion. There was silence in the chapel as the first rays of the rising sun streamed in through the windows. The wolf whined softly, then lay down, curling its tail over its face. He slept, and Artemis tiptoed out, know his transition would come with the sunlight.

Artemis rode up to the garden of the Franciscan monastery in Ravello and looked down the cliffs at the bay. She stayed there, revolving her thoughts until the sun had fully risen. It had been a long night. When the sunlight spread across the lemon groves, she returned to the chapel.

CHAPTER 30

THE REQUEST

The sun was fully up and Brother Faunus was gazing down at the emerald bay when Artemis cut the Ducati's single-cylinder engine. He turned and greeted her warmly.

"I see you've procured your own transportation!"

"I grew up riding. My dad rode an Indian. He started me out on a little Vespa. I still drive my Harley Sportser to campus when the weather is nice."

The requisite pleasantries dispensed with, Faunus assumed a serious, determined tone.

"Artemis, you recall of course that you initially came to Italy to give a talk on the Lycanthrope of Ravello, the werewolf, at the Castel Nuovo in Naples."

"I do indeed, but the best-laid plans..."

"No. It's more important than ever that you give that talk, only not at the palace. You must give it here, at the chapel."

"How do you propose to bring the convocation of history scholars down here and fit them in this space?"

"It wouldn't be for the scholars. It would be for the lemon farmers, the shepherds and goatherds, the donkey drivers, the villagers here on the Monti Lattari."

"Wow. Okay. How much credibility does a Sarah Lawrence professor have with them?"

"I will take care of that. I'm from the Bronx, but these are my people now. I see my own ancestors in their faces. The calluses on their hands are the calluses of my forebears going back for generations, long before we were Americans. I know them, and they know me. Trust me on this."

"I do trust you, Faunus. If this will help you and help them, then that's what I came here to do. Just give me some direction."

"Take today to relax at the seashore. Consider the tarot card, but keep that counsel to yourself. Meditate on the wolf of Gubbio, and Francis's brilliant bit of interspecies diplomacy. Put that together in plain speech, and I will translate it word for word for the villagers. This little chapel has for centuries been a place where the Franciscan friars would make announcements to their parishioners. Tomorrow morning, we will revive that tradition. I will get the word around today."

He put an encouraging hand on her shoulder.

"I will introduce you as a seer, a sibyl from America. A woman possessing the second sight, the ability to see and communicate with spirits. They will all understand, and they will listen with respect."

"But…"

"Before you stop me, Artemis, every word of that is true. Now go, take the day and relax. I will introduce you tomorrow at full sunrise. The moon is on the wane, and it's time to allay their fears."

He turned and walked into the whitewashed chapel.

CHAPTER 31

THE LYCANTHROPE OF RAVELLO

Trying to clear her mind in order to find the right words to say to the villagers, Artemis rode the ferry to Positano, where she shopped at the mile-long flea market stretching up the ancient stairway to the cliffs above the town. As Brother Faunus said, there were always stairs on the Amalfi Peninsula. Then she boarded a tiny fishing boat that ferried her to a secluded beach, where she dined on fresh-caught branzino and began composing her address to the villagers.

Back at the Hotel Croce, Artemis slept soundly until her travel alarm went off. She was still exhausted from the previous all-night pursuit across the hills. When the sun was fully risen, she rode the motorcycle slowly back up the ridge and joined the villagers gathered on the cut grass in front of the chapel. Oleander and grapevines marked a natural border, creating a small sort of amphitheater. Brother Faunus came out of the chapel and raised his hand to give the blessing. The listeners assembled themselves, families standing together, answering with *amen*s at the proper places. Their heads were bowed in pious respect for the setting and the Franciscan brother. After a moment of silence he spoke, first in English and then in Italian.

"We have an honored guest who has traveled all the way from America to bring peace to our community. She is a seer, a sibyl, and she possesses the second sight."

Murmurs among the assembled, then silence.

"What's more, she has spoken with the Lycanthrope."

Exclamations of *"Dio di benedica!"* Many in the crowd made the sign of the cross on their breasts. Some fingered rosary beads.

"I will end my remarks now and introduce to you Signorina Artemis Fletcher, a doctor of history."

Faunus stood aside as Artemis began to speak, in English. She paused after each phrase while he translated into Italian.

"I was summoned here to your beautiful mountains and seacoast in the hope that I might communicate with a creature...a creature around whom an atmosphere of fear and uncertainty has been engendered. A wolf is indeed a powerful and fearsome beast, and throughout history it has been in a posture of counterpose, of enmity, with man. A wolf may feed on sheep and goats. Those things are natural to the wolf. They indicate no malevolent emotion on the part of the animal toward man. A wolf who lives near this place, in this district known the world over for agricultural richness, will indeed be seen by many as a threat to livestock, a threat to the very things that make Amalfi great. Beyond that, old beliefs may make even darker claims about the creature's origins and intentions. I came here with all of that knowledge at the forefront of my thoughts, but I also kept my mind and heart open like the blue sky above, which doesn't pass judgment on the birds who fly through it."

She paused, making eye contact with her listeners, who ranged in age from toddlers to the elderly.

"We are part of nature as well. No one knew that more or felt it more deeply in his soul more than Saint Francis, the patron of animals. He was called many centuries ago to the town of Gubbio in Umbria. A wolf was heard howling under the full moon. As you know, Saint Francis called the moon his sister, and he sensed that the wolf must have felt a fraternal love for the same sister. Thus, Francis and the wolf were brothers. He met with the wolf under the full moon, and together they agreed that if the townspeople were to feed the wolf food that would otherwise be thrown away, the entrails and other unused parts of fish and slaughtered livestock, the wolf would leave off from any threat to their pastured and domestic animals. In the end, the townspeople treated the wolf as a brother, and they lived their lives in mutual peace."

She paused again, and spoke with an intensified sincerity.

"I met with your wolf, under the full moon two nights ago."

More cries of *"Dio di benedica!"*

"I communicated with the wolf. I was in no danger. We agreed that if you, the villagers who farm these hills, will accept the pact of Saint Francis, with the blessing of Brother Faunus, who wears the woolen robe, triple-knotted cincture, and sandals in honor of the saint, then you and your brother wolf can live your lives in mutual peace and safety.

"There is an ancient hermit's hut, the abode of a holy man long ago, on the cliffs above the footpath leading up from the Schiato ravine toward Bomerano. It is a humble place, long blessed by the piety of the men who lived alone there, praying without cease. If three days' provisions are left there, and the hut is undisturbed during every full moon, the wolf will abide by the pact of his brother Francis, and your livestock will not be threatened. You will still hear the wolf, high on the ridge, but remember that he is singing a song of praise to his sister in the sky. With that I will take my leave, offering my sincere thanks for your hospitality and your kindness in listening to my story."

Brother Faunus stepped forward and offered a blessing for the pact of Saint Francis, closing with *"Vade in pace."*

CHAPTER 32

BUON VIAGGO

The ferryboat whistle blew the final "all aboard." Artemis turned on the gangway and took one last look at Amalfi and the mountains rising up from the idyllic seacoast. She would travel by sea to Salerno, then by train to Naples, onward to Rome, and finally to the airport for her flight to the States. Somehow, Amalfi seemed like reality, and the world to which she was returning just a dream. She waved a last goodbye to Brother Faunus, standing by the beat-up Lancia. Like his patron saint, he was a man who appeared humble and simple but was infinitely complex in ways that only Artemis could know and understand. She wondered if they would ever meet again.

Later, high above the North Atlantic, thoughts and images ran through her head like scenes on film at thirty frames per second. Brother Faunus, Alistair Wulver, Saint Francis, the old forest god Faunus, and Sky Woman, the Virgin above the altar, her own namesake Artemis the Wild Huntress. The chain of interconnecting souls were links that spanned centuries. How did she fit in to that shape-shifting lineage? *Maybe*, she thought, looking down at the emerald sea, *it's like the ocean, where no single wave knows how vast the whole is.*

It was the nodding god of sleep, Morpheus, who finally calmed her racing mind. She woke to the pilot's voice announcing their approach into Kennedy Airport and home.

Strabo had sent a limo to transport her home to Westchester, and as the car turned west on the Long Island Expressway and the Manhattan skyline came into view, the familiar surroundings of New York knit together the unraveled threads of the past few days. Artemis yawned, and turned her thoughts to a quiet evening, trading tales of adventure with Tunde.

PART FOUR

Summer in the City

CHAPTER 33

THE VILLAGE

Back in Westchester, Artemis and Ayotunde compared notes on their solo adventures in Italy and Nigeria, and they instituted a temporary ban on sugar after their dousing at Ross Castle. Once their Strabo reports were filed, Artemis looked forward to a relaxing late summer, lounging by the pool at Atalanta, hiking the Westchester carriage roads, and catching up on reading. Ayotunde, on the other hand, had something more energetic in mind. On a humid mid-August afternoon, she asked a question.

"Artemis, do you ever dance?"

"Dance, like the foxtrot?"

"I was thinking of something more like the loco-motion."

"I could probably pull off a sarabande or a bourrée."

"All right, at least you admit that you don't know any music newer than 'Greensleeves.' We're going to have to do something about that."

"Okay, Tunde. Educate me."

"We'll start tomorrow. Remember the Mod clothes we bought back in Dublin? Now's the time to dig them out. Two cups of coffee in the morning, then we'll catch the train."

At Grand Central, they transferred to the subway down to the 4th Street Station in the heart of Greenwich Village. From there they walked east, with Ayotunde acting as tour guide.

"First stop, Washington Square!"

They strolled for a block on 4th Street, where they caught sight of the great arch overlooking a marble fountain surrounded by a celebratory cross section of the city's population. Everyone was enjoying the sunshine, to the soundtrack of music coming from all points of the compass. Ayotunde began pointing out musicians, along with members of the motley crew of Greenwich Village characters who created the festival-like atmosphere. Fortune tellers, crystal ball readers, and declamatory poets mingled with bongo players and strongmen flexing their muscles. Marble benches lined a central area around the fountain, where ad hoc jam sessions sprang up, creating a joyous cacophony. Walking around the circle in the square was a moveable feast of different sounds and styles.

"Over there is Sun Ra. He's an avant-garde jazz musician. He plays on Mondays at a place called Slug's. He says that he's traveled around the solar system, and that provides him with his inspiration."

"Wow, Tunde. This is fascinating. I've been down to this part of town to give lectures at the university, but I never ventured into the Village. I always thought it just wasn't a place where I could fit in."

"It's a place where anybody fits in! Look around, Artemis. No one is judged down here on their clothes, their skin, their conformity. It's wide open. That's why I wanted to bring you to the Village. Now, let's hit MacDougal Street, and then maybe a club or two."

"Lead the way!" Artemis was getting into the spirit.

They exited the park at the southwest corner, weaving between the spectators who followed the local chess masters. Two blocks south, where an alleyway known as Minetta Lane branched off of MacDougal, a roaring, soulful blues guitar was erupting from a corner nightclub. The marquee out front announced the next event.

Cafe Wha

Live Music Nightly 'til ???

Tonight:

Jimmy James and the Blue Flames

"Fletch, I'll introduce you to Jimmy someday. He's an amazing musician, but it might be a little raucous for someone more accustomed to lute music."

"Hey, give me a break. I'm getting more beatnik by the minute!"

They stopped for coffee on the east side of MacDougal at the Kettle of Fish. A musician was playing a flamenco piece on guitar. He was leaning over the instrument, listening intently, showing no inclination to ingratiate himself to the coffee-and-wine-drinking audience. A basket was being passed among the patrons. Artemis and Ayotunde each put in a dollar.

Reinforced with strong Turkish coffee, they rejoined the nighttime throng outside. They turned left at the next corner and made their way down Bleecker Street to the Village Gate. They sat at a tiny table, inches away from the next table. The house lights went dark, and a single spotlight shone down on a woman seated at the piano. Ayotunde took a deep breath and closed her eyes as Nina Simone sang "Black Is the Color of My True Love's Hair," an old Irish air, reinvented in the voice of an American Black woman. She dug deep into her soul, and when she was finished, some in the audience remained silent, not wanting to interrupt the moment by applauding. Artemis was moved, too. She had never heard anything like it, and there was something about the singer that reminded her of the women who had appeared to her at times of danger, in Nepal, Italy, and Japan, women who were partially or wholly ethereal spirits, able to move freely between different forms. In the lone spotlight, Nina Simone seemed transfigured like them.

Back on the street, Ayotunde suggested that they visit a few landmark Greenwich Village bars. Artemis was enjoying the sights and sounds, and she was agreeable to anything her companion suggested. Just down the block from the Village Gate, there was a corner bar called the Back Fence. The sandwich board out front read in chalk:

Live Music Tonight

Farrell and Kennedy

No Cover

Artemis ordered a seltzer and they listened to a few songs by the two guitar-playing singers. When they came down from the tiny stage, she had a few questions for them.

"How often do you guys perform here?"

Farrell was laconic.

"Wednesdays nine to one."

"I don't see a basket going around. Does the bar owner actually pay you?"

"Oh yeah," Kennedy answered enthusiastically. "Five bucks each!"

"That's all?"

"No. We also get a burger! It's great to have a steady gig on Bleecker Street."

Artemis was contemplating the thought of living on a weekly salary of five dollars and a hamburger when Ayotunde suggested they stop in next door, at another small bar called the Tin Angel.

A lissome blond guitarist was singing about the cycles of life, using the metaphor of a carousel.

Artemis whispered to Ayotunde, "Those Back Fence guys were okay, but this is more to my taste."

"She's fairly new in town. They say she's from out west in Canada."

When Joni Mitchell finished singing the "Circle Game" song, as she called it, Artemis and Ayotunde continued on their rounds. Ayotunde grabbed Artemis's jacket cuff and shook it.

"Hey, you! You still haven't danced!"

"Well, you haven't taught me how."

"There's nothing to teach! You just let the music move you. I think we need to drop in at the Night Owl. We can dance there."

The Lovin' Spoonful were tuning up as the two women sat down. John Sebastian noticed Ayotunde and came over to the table. He had sideburns, wore a striped French navy jersey and round wire-rimmed glasses, and had an engagingly crooked smile.

"Tunde! It's great to see you. Been out of town?"

"Yeah, just a little trip to Ireland and Nigeria."

"On the road again, sure as you're born!"

John returned to the stage, and as the band started up, Artemis overcame any dance floor shyness. When they broke into "Do You Believe in Magic," she decided she did, in fact, believe in magic.

After the Spoonful finished their set, Fletch and Tunde walked across MacDougal Street into Washington Square. As they passed the statue of Garibaldi, they caught sight of another eccentric Village character. He was leading a small band of men dressed as pirates with tricorn hats. They were heading east across the square. Artemis was about to break into a laugh when Ayotunde pulled her aside, behind the statue.

"He's bad news. Don't even make eye contact."

"What's his story? A trip around the solar system?"

"Nothing so benevolent. He calls himself Calico Jack. That in itself would just be quirky, but he actually believes he is the real Calico Jack."

"There's a real Calico Jack?"

"There was. When I first heard about this guy, his name piqued my curiosity. I went to our campus library and looked it up. There *was* a real Calico Jack. He was an actual pirate, John Rackham, who operated around New York harbor back in the early 1700s. His territory ranged all the way down to Jamaica and the Bahamas. In Nassau, a woman named Anne Bonny, the wife of a British spy, switched sides and ran off with Rackham on his pirate ship. She took enthusiastic part in raiding law-abiding merchant ships. No one knows the full record of their crimes, but they got careless and started throwing parties outside the safety of their hideout in the Bahamas. The captain and crew were all drinking rum off of Jamaica when the British caught up with them. They hanged Calico Jack at Gallows Point and displayed him at the entrance to the harbor as a message to his criminal cronies."

"And Anne Bonny?"

"She disappeared from history. Might have died in prison, might have been hanged, might have escaped. In any case, this small-time crook who just strode past us is convinced he's the heir, or maybe the reincarnation, of John Rackham, aka Calico Jack. He practices his own brand of piracy on land: burglary, armed robbery, crooked deals of all kinds. He also has an old Chris-Craft Runabout that he souped up like a hot rod. He hides it somewhere in the docks over on the West Side. People say they see him on the river under the moonlight, flying the skull and crossbones."

"So he's a nut."

"A nut yes, but a dangerous one."

CHAPTER 34

THE CEDAR TAVERN

The two women ambled leisurely around the fountain for an hour, soaking up the late Summer sights and sounds. As the crowd began to thin, Ayotunde tugged at Artemis's sleeve.

"Fletch, let's visit a real Village dive bar. No music, just atmosphere. It's a landmark!"

They exited the park at the northeast corner and made their way up University Place to the Cedar Tavern. This had been the hangout, gathering place, and rowdy salon of the abstract expressionist painters a decade before. Now the old rebels were enjoying success out in the Hamptons, but the tavern was still a down and dirty hangout. Ayotunde wove through the crowd and cleared a narrow space at the bar. Philosophy professors and newspaper columnists were arguing the issues of the day.

Artemis was surveying the scene, nursing her second seltzer with lime, when she spotted Calico Jack at the corner table, surrounded by his ragged cohorts. He held a tumbler in his right hand, and with his left fist he was pounding on the table. Even over the noise of the crowd, she could hear him shouting.

"I'm gonna get me Solomon Gundi!"

He repeated the proclamation, even louder.

"I'm gonna get me Solomon Gundi, lads, or this isn't a blackjack of fine Jamaican rum!"

He reared his head back and quaffed deeply. As he started to lower the tumbler, his eye caught sight of Artemis standing at the bar. He froze, arm still in the air. He lowered it slowly and dropped the empty vessel, never taking his gaze off of her. He silenced his madcap crew and slowly advanced. The crowd parted like the Red Sea. Calico Jack stood in front of Artemis and her bemused companion. He straightened his spine and removed his tricorn hat. He placed it over his heart and made a steep, formal bow. Righting himself, he spoke in an oddly antiquated British accent.

"Dear lady, I never thought I would see the day. My last thought as the hangman's noose tightened was of you. Would you follow me to the gallows? Would we ever be reunited? And now, here you are."

He turned to the address the crowded bar.

"Gentlemen," he bowed awkwardly to a table of female university students, "and ladies. I propose a toast!"

The crowd raised their drinks.

"To Anne Bonny, the bravest woman who ever proved her worth on the high seas, under the flag of the Jolly Roger!"

Caught up in the moment, half the crowd shouted "Hurrah!" and drank up. The other half looked around with raised eyebrows, some glancing with sympathy at Artemis, the apparent object of his misplaced tribute.

Artemis turned to Ayotunde and whispered, "What the heck is going on?"

Ayotunde shrugged.

"Just humor him?" The statement had a question mark.

"I've humored him too much already. Let's get out of here."

As they made their way out on to the street, they heard Calico Jack shouting again. His meaning was still cryptic.

"I'm gonna get me Solomon Gundi!"

He was still repeating it as they turned the corner on 12th Street and headed back toward MacDougal.

"Artemis, let's get something to eat while we try to relax after that bit of weirdness. I think we need a real Greenwich Village pizza."

They found a table at John's on Bleecker Street. The busboy wiped it down with his rag, then laid down two glasses of tap water and two menus.

A few minutes later the waiter arrived.

"Any beverages tonight, ladies?"

Artemis didn't look up from her study of the menu. From years of scholarly research, she had developed a habit of reading slowly and meticulously, scanning for details, and that applied to menus as well as textbooks.

"Water's fine, thanks."

"I'll give you a few minutes, then, and keep in mind, we don't serve slices at John's, only whole pies."

He walked away, and Artemis looked up. She recognized the voice, but he had disappeared into the kitchen.

Five minutes later, the waiter returned. She looked up this time.

"Oh my gosh…"

Ayotunde reached across the table.

"Are you okay, Fletch?"

"Yes. Ayotunde, allow me to introduce Brother Faunus."

CHAPTER 35

THE PRODIGAL SON

Brother Faunus wiped his hands on a towel tucked into his apron.

"I get off at midnight. I'll be at Caffe Reggio. Nice to meet you, Ayotunde."

Much later, over cups of espresso at the cafe, he told his story.

"I had to leave Italy. After your address, Artemis, the Franciscans up the hill in Ravello started to connect the dots with what you said and my going missing every month for three days. I had to get back to New York to figure out who I am. I left the order."

He glanced at Ayotunde, then back at Artemis.

"Does she know?"

"She knows about my trip to Amalfi. She understands. Trust me on that."

"Okay."

"Where are you living?"

"On the Bowery."

"What address?"

"No address. Literally on the Bowery. On the street."

"Is your name still Brother Faunus?"

"I don't have a name. My name at John's is Vince Brunetti. That was my name growing up on Arthur Avenue."

"Then that's your name."

"No. Vince Brunetti drowned on the Raquette River. I don't know who I am."

"Okay, you're coming with us. You can call John's and quit in the morning. First we need to get you settled in a place to live, and then we'll figure out a name and take it from there."

"Really, you don't have to do this for me."

"Yes I do. Simple as that. Consider it a promise I made to someone a long time ago."

The three of them walked around the corner to the 4th Street subway station and began the rail journey out to Valhalla.

CHAPTER 36

A HOME

At Atalanta, Artemis showed Faunus the back cottage. She gave him the key.

"Let yourself in. There are jeans your size, T-shirts, and some work clothes, a white shirt and chinos, a couple of pairs of shoes. They were left by..." She hesitated. "The previous tenant."

"How can I thank you?"

"Come up to the kitchen in the morning, and we'll figure out getting you settled here."

In the morning, Artemis, Faunus, and Ayotunde waited until the coffee pot was done percolating. Ayotunde poured three cups, and they sat at the table.

"Faunus, do you remember Kevin Macduff at Strabo? He can expedite identification for you. This is your address now. Don't worry about money for the moment. Money is not a problem for me, and it's not a problem for you while you're under my protection. There is employment for you out here in Westchester. Now, your name..."

"If I have one, I don't know what it is."

"All right then. Your spirit guide was Saint Francis. Even though you left the order, you are still connected to nature in a unique way, one might say, so I suggest Francis Faunus. Let's keep part of your old name. Francis Vincent Faunus. Any objections?"

Faunus smiled wanly and shrugged.

"Okay with me."

"That will work for your ID, but I'm still going to call you Faunus!"

She grew serious.

"Now, you know we have to talk about the moon. At the dark of the moon, we'll walk you over to Cranberry Lake, a quiet place in the woods nearby. It's a lovely area, with a huge dam and reservoir, and a forest trail that no one travels after nightfall. You can reach it from the cottage without going out on the street. The trail leads to an abandoned granite quarry. Your only company will be foxes, raccoons, and otters in the flooded pit. There are caves, secluded places. You'll be safe there when the full moon comes around again."

Faunus got cleaned up and dressed in time to ride with his protectors over to the Warner Library in Tarrytown. It was there that they introduced him to Dido Parren.

CHAPTER 37

DIDO PARREN

Dido Parren worked as a docent at the library. She couldn't commit to a full-time position because her first obligation was to the *Tarrytown Daily News*. She'd been promoted to an editor's desk there after discovering and publishing, as a cub reporter, the location of the lycanthrope, the wolverine who was hiding in plain sight just up the road in Scarborough. Coincidentally, she was also friends with Alistair Wulver, although she knew him as Alex Wolf, right up until the day he retired as head librarian. She never knew that Alex and the wolverine were one and the same creature.

Dido didn't accept pay at the library, but she rose through the ranks and became interim director after Alistair's departure. Among other things, she was in charge of hiring and firing, and she knew and trusted Artemis Fletcher.

"Dido, great to see you! You look terrific! You remember Ayotunde Ibukun?"

"Of course. You two haven't been in for a while. Traveling?"

"Oh, we had a couple of little trips. Dido, this is Frank Faunus. He recently left the Franciscan order, where he served parishioners in Italy. He's an expert not only in theology but also mythology, comparative religions, and esoteric traditions. He's also an avid outdoorsman, but I'll let him speak for himself."

While Faunus sat for his interview, Artemis and Ayotunde spent an hour hiking on the Old Croton Aqueduct trail, just up the hill from Broadway in Tarrytown. When they returned, he was sitting on a bench in Patriot's Park, adjacent to the library.

"Well, it looks like I have a job. No more slinging pizza! Nonfiction librarian at the Warner Library. Dido grew up in Astoria, Queens, a Greek neighborhood, and I grew up on Arthur Avenue, an Italian neighborhood, so we talked about how Tarrytown is a bit like a Mediterranean village, sloping down to the waterfront, like my little parish back in Amalfi. I do miss Italy, but I'm already starting to feel at home here in Westchester."

Artemis was glad to hear him coming back to his old talkative self. That was a good sign.

"We've got bikes that will get you back and forth to work. Now, that's enough logistics for a summer day. Let's get something to eat up at Tappan Hill."

CHAPTER 38

THE ISLAND CASTLE

The remainder of the summer passed peacefully. The exciting news was that Olorin, the young artist who was discovered by Ayotunde in Nigeria, moved to Westchester in time to register for her scholarship enrollment at Sarah Lawrence. Ayotunde made use of her Strabo connection, and Kevin Macduff called in a favor at the American Consulate in Lagos to fly Olorin out of the war-torn country on a diplomatic visa. Safely ensconced in campus housing, she frequently rode the bus out to Valhalla to spend afternoons at the estate, working on her English and becoming an unofficial assistant to Ayotunde for her African studies program. Artemis, Ayotunde, Faunus, and Olorin made field trips to New Paltz, where they hiked the rocky Gunks, and to Woodstock, where they took in concerts and lectures at the Byrdcliffe Colony. They explored the Old Dutch Cemetery in Sleepy Hollow, and one day they trekked up the steep trail to Breakneck Ridge, overlooking the Hudson and the mysterious castle on Pollepel Island. Artemis knew the story behind it.

"There was a fellow named Frank Bannerman. He was born in Ireland, came over as a kid around the time of the famine. He was industrious, and he hatched an idea. At the end of the Civil War, he went to auctions and bought all the surplus guns, ammunition, cannons, dynamite, et cetera. He also bought backpacks, boots, and all sorts of things that he could sell to the public. He was buying up surplus after subsequent wars at the Brooklyn Navy Yard, and by the time he'd accumulated millions of rounds of ammo, there was nowhere he could safely store it in New York City. He bought this island and built a castle to live in and a massive stone warehouse, like a medieval keep. As you can guess, things eventually started to explode, and the boat that ferried Bannerman and his clients out to the island sank. The place was abandoned and has just been sitting there. I've heard talk that the state might buy it, probably just to keep curious idiots from going out there. Here, look through the binoculars."

The spyglasses were passed around. It was a spooky ruin, with an OFF-LIMITS sign at the old boat landing bearing emphatic warnings of danger.

After a time, the four hikers finished their picnic and returned to the Jeep, parked on Route 90 near the riverside.

The rest of the summer and early fall passed that way, with outings and occasional trips into the city to hear music. Artemis was quickly becoming a fan of contemporary folk singers and modern jazz. She even started building a collection of new stereo album releases: John Coltrane's *Ascension* and Herbie Hancock's *Maiden Voyage* alternated with Ayotunde's current favorites, the Beach Boys' *Pet Sounds* and of course Nina Simone's *Wild Is the Wind*. Classes resumed on campus, and life assumed a patina of normalcy. Of course that could only last until the next phone call from Kevin Macduff. That came on October 28, 1966.

PART FIVE

The Case of the Purloined Painting

CHAPTER 39

THE MACDUFF CALL

"Artemis, Kevin Macduff here. I wonder if you and Ayotunde could meet me down at the Strabo Club around five. I want to take you to dinner downtown and discuss a mission."

"Great, Kevin, but as far as a mission is concerned, you know we're in mid-semester at Sarah Lawrence. We don't have a break for another month."

"No sweat. This mission is last minute, just for tonight, and it's right here in New York City."

"Got it. See you there!"

CHAPTER 40

THE CLUB

Kevin Macduff was waiting under the awning at the front door of the Strabo Society when the Jeep pulled up. He jumped in the back seat and greeted Artemis and Ayotunde.

"We're heading downtown, Fifth Avenue and 12th Street, southeast corner."

Artemis found a parking spot on 12th, and they walked around the corner to an imposing brownstone. The front stoop was flanked by wrought-iron railings that created a narrow porch in front of tall casement windows. A bell rang somewhere in the building when Macduff pushed the door open. A dapper man, dressed in a navy blue suit and a diamond point bow tie, greeted them in the entrance foyer. He pumped Macduff's hand.

"Kevin, so glad you could come!"

He turned to Artemis and Ayotunde and bowed slightly.

"Welcome to the Salmagundi Club."

He paused while they looked around. Art was everywhere. Oil paintings hung on every wall, sculptures were mounted on pedestals, and a marble fireplace was guarded by two bas-relief caryatids. The sculpted women seemed to say, *This place is grand. Take your time and look at everything around you.*

The man introduced himself.

"My name is Martin Hartley. I am currently club president."

He gestured, sweeping around the room.

"The Salmagundi Club was founded nearly a century ago by artists. The members not only relax, do research, and network with like-minded souls here; they display their work in our annual series of themed exhibitions. We have a permanent archive not only of paintings, but of nineteenth-century books dealing with fine art as well. All of the art displayed at the club is representational. Abstract is, of course, well curated by other galleries in the city. Now, follow me downstairs for some quick refreshment."

The lower level was a casual space set up for lounging about. Heavy, rough-hewn ceiling beams suggested a European pub. Plaster gargoyles leered down from the corners.

Hartley called out from behind the bar.

"Tea, beer?"

The women chose the former, Macduff the latter.

While they sipped, the trio of visitors had a chance to peruse their surroundings. One wall was covered with wooden palettes, the kind on which artists mix their colors. These particular palettes had been turned into impromptu canvases. Various painters had created works on them, painting right on the original kidney-bean shape, working around the cutouts for their thumb and fingers.

"You can see from looking around that we are not overly formal or stuffy here."

Hartley continued talking while he collected the empty glassware.

"Upstairs in the library we have a collection of painted mugs. They make a unique sort of record of our membership. We feel that their styles tell more about them than names on a printed list. We like to think of ourselves as a sketch club, an archive of spontaneous self-expression, and that brings me to our upcoming exhibit, which opens at one o'clock Sunday. Let's continue on to the Grand Gallery upstairs, and I will fill you in."

They followed Hartley up to the main floor, and then up a wide stairway. Artemis noted that he was now carrying a folded copy of *The New York Times* under his left arm. He talked as they climbed to the upper level.

"Sunday is the opening of our annual thumb box exhibition. A thumb box is a small wooden box in which an artist can carry basic colors and brushes and a small canvas. It's a portable kit for plein air excursions to the outdoors. Because the box and the canvas are small, the resulting painting is small. We have the premier collection of these diminutive works. To stand in a gallery full of them is to be surrounded by charm. One feels the vivacity of painting quickly in the open air. The thumb box show has been one of our most popular exhibitions since the first one was mounted in 1908."

They came to two large oak doors. Hartley pulled the right-hand door open, and they entered the gallery. A multipaned skylight took up most of the ceiling space so that the paintings were lit by natural light. They were indeed small. They invited a closer look, and Hartley led the group clockwise around the room, commenting now and then on an artist, a location, or a technique. The last painting on their circuit, as they neared the oak door again, was cloaked in a black canvas wrap.

"We like to boast about our more distinguished members. Sadly, we lost one, Winston Churchill, in January of last year. We lost another one just recently, and that is why I have asked you to meet me here today."

He carefully lifted the canvas, exposing a tiny painting, smaller that a sheet of onion-skin paper. It was a naturalistic picture of an imposing mountain. At its foot a wide river flowed. The background was a fiery sunset, streaked with shades of orange and red. It was remarkably powerful for such a small work.

"You recognize this piece as Barbizon school, of course, but I prefer to think of it as an example of the current revival of interest in the Hudson River school. I confess to a streak of regionalism when it comes to landscapes."

Hartley studied the canvas thoughtfully for a moment.

"It's a lovely painting, to be sure, but in this case the subject is less important than the artist. I don't imagine you scan the obituaries in the *Times* every day, but if you did so yesterday, you would have read this half-page article."

He unfolded the newspaper. It was open to the obituaries. Hartley held it where they could read the top headline: ART WORLD GIANT HOBART TYLER DEAD AT EIGHTY-SIX.

Artemis spoke first.

"Let me guess. This painting is by Hobart Tyler."

"Correct. When this work came into our collection, he was healthy as one of his horses out in Southampton. He still seemed to be so when we mounted the painting this week in anticipation of the opening Sunday. You read the headline. His pieces had been selling at auction for half a million, but as of yesterday, that value has doubled, maybe even more than doubled, because this was custom painted by Tyler for us, and there have never been prints or copies made. I would go so far as to say that, at this moment, *Bear Mountain at Sunset* is priceless."

Macduff spoke for the first time since they entered the gallery.

"So what's our role in all of this?"

"Kevin, we are a casual sketch club. We have never in our history hired security for one of our exhibitions. We're open to the public for four hours each afternoon, and while we keep an eye on things, we've never had this kind of conjunction of timing and value. Frankly, it's dangerous to have this painting displayed this way, but we can't simply pull it off the wall. We have to consider Tyler's family and his legacy. To be honest, we need a guard, like the ones at the Met. Just for tonight, until Pinkerton can send a crew tomorrow."

"What about the NYPD?"

"No crime has been committed, yet. It's the weekend before Halloween, and they are not going to assign uniformed officers to a crime scene that's only anticipated by a nervous curator like myself."

Macduff set his jaw.

"Martin, you know me as director of the Strabo Society, but I'm also a retired Westchester cop. I don't wear the uniform anymore, but I can stand guard at the front door tonight, with a pot of strong coffee, if that will ease your mind."

"That would indeed ease my mind. My staff are culinary workers and art historians. I can't ask them to be security guards as well."

"Consider it done. Artemis and Ayotunde, I need you to be my backup. Halloween weekend is crazy down here in Greenwich Village. Anything could happen. Cover the streets between here and Bleecker, and check back frequently. I'll be on the front stoop all night, just to indicate that there's a security presence on the premises. I don't anticipate trouble, but on the force we used to say 'Expect the worst and hope for the best.' Now, Martin, the only recompense I ask is that you lead the three of us in the direction of that cooking aroma wafting up from the dining room."

Hartley looked relieved.

"In that case, please join me for dinner downstairs, before I lock up and hand the keys over to Kevin, our new praetorian guard."

As they descended the wide stairs, Artemis had one more question.

"*Salmagundi* is an unusual word. What's the origin of the club's name?"

"As I mentioned, we like to think of ourselves as spontaneous and freewheeling. Salmagundi is from an old French culinary word for a hodgepodge, a motley combination. European sailors brought it to the Caribbean back in the eighteenth century."

Hartley chuckled and continued in a lighthearted vein.

"There was even a rum drink down in Jamaica called the Solomon Gundi."

Ayotunde stopped in her tracks for a moment, then continued down the stairs. She elbowed Artemis and silently mouthed the words *"I'm gonna get me Solomon Gundi."*

The two women begged off from dinner. They assured Hartley and Macduff that they would be close by, then exited by the front door. They stood on the narrow porch.

"Artemis, you remember where we've heard that before. At the Cedar Tavern last summer, the night that Calico Jack was convinced that you were his sidekick Anne Bonny."

"I remember that we got out of there on the double."

Ayotunde was breathless.

"Yes, but as we were leaving, he shouted those exact words again to his drunken crew. 'I'm gonna get me Solomon Gundi.' If that's an eighteenth century Jamaican sailors' drink, then no one else, even here in New York, would use that expression, and it means…Salmagundi."

"Okay. I'm convinced. It seems we now have a suspect for a crime that hasn't even happened yet. How do we find him in time to stop it?"

"I say we start at the Cedar Tavern."

CHAPTER 41

THE GAME IS AFOOT

Grace Church was ringing the six o'clock Angelus as the two sleuths raced one block over and down from the Salmagundi Club, to 11th Street and University Place. The Cedar Tavern stood on the corner. The room was filled shoulder to shoulder with students, tourists, and Village denizens, dressed in an anarchic array of Halloween regalia. They scanned the crowd. No tricorn pirate headgear in evidence. They pushed through the crush to the bar, which the bartender was wiping down with his rag.

"Excuse me!"

Artemis shouted again over the merrymaking din.

"Excuse me, is Calico Jack around?"

"Calico who?"

"Calico Jack."

"Never heard of him."

"He's a regular customer."

"Like I said, I never heard of him, and if I had heard of him, he ain't here."

"We just need to talk to him."

He put down his rag and looked her in the eye for the first time.

"Look, I get wives, girlfriends, private detectives, and who-knows-who in here every night looking for my regulars. You wanna know why they're my regulars? Because if anybody asks, I never heard of 'em!"

He picked up his rag.

"Now if you'll excuse me, I got a full house of paying customers."

CHAPTER 42

THE WHITE HORSE TAVERN

Not quite one mile west, at six o'clock, on the corner of 11th and Hudson Streets, Calico Jack didn't hear the ringing of the Angelus. He was leading his crew in a crescendo of toasts celebrating his real and imagined criminal coups. He had held his rum well enough to leap onto the round tabletop.

"Tonight, lads, I get me Solomon Gundi!"

This was met with a general drunken roar of approval.

"And if the king has stationed a guard to watch over my treasure, I'll ply him with my Liverpool punch!"

More roaring.

"And then we'll see him go down with his arms at his sides and his rifle at attention, as ordered by King George himself!"

A barrage of bellows.

He crouched down, still on the tabletop, put a finger to his lips, and whispered sotto voce.

"Now lads, look sharp! This treasure is mine alone, but once I have it secured, we'll have collateral to bargain with any crew in this city, any crew in the world! But keep silent while I do my work. You will hear from me when the plan is complete. In the meantime…"

He raised his voice.

"Rum all around for this lot!"

While they shouted, sang, and toasted, Calico Jack slipped out the side door of the White Horse Tavern, straightened his tricorn hat, and joined the Halloween revelers heading east on 11th Street, in the direction of the Salmagundi Club.

CHAPTER 43

THE LIVERPOOL PUNCH

Artemis and Ayotunde stood outside the Cedar Tavern, scanning around as if their quarry might simply be strolling down 11th Street.

"Well, we can't just stand here. We're just a few blocks up from Washington Square. That seems like the logical place to start looking."

As they crossed 11th Street, heading toward the square, Calico Jack was in fact strolling down 11th Street, one block west of them. As they turned south on University Place, he turned north onto Fifth Avenue.

Under the Washington Square arch, a stage was set up on the back of a flatbed truck. Sun Ra and his band, the Solar Arkestra, were leading the audience in a chant: "Next stop Jupiter!"

The crowd was engaged in a sort of communal revel, each dancer improvising their own movements. The aggregation created a kind of living organism, moving to the rhythm of the chant. The scene was surreal, and yet it fit right into the human mosaic of Greenwich Village.

"Wow, Ayotunde, is this jazz?"

"This is more than jazz, Artemis. This is something deeper. This is Africa."

They pulled themselves away from the hypnotic scene. They were on a mission to find a criminal and somehow waylay him *before* he committed a crime. They had to scan the celebration without being drawn into it. They were looking for a tricorn hat.

After a full hour, an hour that took them through the park, down MacDougal, and across Bleecker all the way to Broadway, they looked at their watches. It was seven o'clock. They agreed that it was time to check on Macduff back at the Salmagundi Club. When they reached the corner of Fifth Avenue and 12th Street, they exchanged anxious looks. There was no one on the front stoop. They rushed up the steps and almost tripped over Macduff, crumpled on the porch. He seemed to be in a deep sleep. Artemis took his pulse—normal. She checked his breathing—also normal. An empty open bottle of Myers's Rum lay next to him.

"Tunde, he's not just passed out. There's something else going on here."

She knelt down, picked up the bottle, and sniffed the cap threads. She withdrew quickly.

"For a bottle of straight rum, this smells a lot like fruit. Could be a homebrew Jamaican punch, but…"

She sniffed again and crinkled her nose.

"Pears. Smells like pears. Chloral hydrate is my best guess. Knockout drops. They used to use it to drug sailors in taverns. Poor fellows would wake up at sea. Tunde, here's a quick detective lesson in case you run up against this again."

She held the bottle up toward Ayotunde.

"Take a whiff, but just be quick. You don't want to drug yourself. Try to store that pear smell in your memory."

Ayotunde sniffed the bottle.

"Okay, now see if you can find hot sauce somewhere in the neighborhood. We need to wake Kevin up and see if he recalls who dosed him."

Ayotunde ran full speed down the block and found a corner deli. The man behind the counter was reading a racing form. He didn't look up while she caught her breath.

"Excuse me, sir."

She took another breath, slowing down.

"Do you carry hot sauce?"

The man finally looked up from his race handicapping.

"Do we carry hot sauce? What kind of pepper you lookin' for? We got cayenne, habanero, jalapeño, New Mexico green…"

Ayotunde had gotten her breath back. She dropped the formalities and shouted: "I don't care! What's the hottest?"

The man raised an eyebrow.

"Well, lady, that all depends on one's taste buds, but if you want the original…"

He reached back to the shelves behind his stool, then turned and banged a small bottle down on the counter. It was red with a white label, and green plastic tape securing a red cap.

"Tabasco. That's the stuff. The original. From Avery Island, Louisiana."

"Fine. Great, I'll take it. Thanks!"

Ayotunde slapped two dollars on the counter and ran out of the shop.

Artemis administered the antidote like smelling salts, waving the open bottle under Kevin's nose. Slowly, he began to come around. The two women propped him up on his elbows.

The first words he mumbled were, "That pirate."

"Kevin, you're going to be all right once you wake up. Can you tell me the last thing you remember?"

"Artemis, what are you doing here? Where am I?"

"Somebody slipped you a mickey, Kevin. Who was it?"

He sat up. He was starting to get his bearings.

"Oh man. The pirate. There was a bunch of costumed people going by. It was like a parade. Like trick-or-treaters, but grown-ups. A clown tossed me a Snickers bar. I guess I got caught up in the spirit a little bit. There was a pirate hoisting a bottle. He offered me a swig of his punch. In fact, he gave me the whole bottle."

He rubbed his eyes, waking up a little more.

"I figured a little nip wouldn't do any harm. Y'know, a taste of rum punch to celebrate Halloween? That's the last thing I remember."

"Okay, let's try standing up."

Kevin found his feet and took a deep breath. He patted his pockets.

"Oh my gosh, the front door key. It's gone!"

The door was unlocked. Kevin grabbed his flashlight, and they raced up the wide stairway. The gallery door was open, and where Hobart Tyler's *Bear Mountain at Sunset* was hanging only a few hours earlier, there was only empty space. The painting was gone.

CHAPTER 44

CAFFE REGGIO

They convened on the front porch of the club. Kevin was looking sheepish. Artemis laid both of her hands on his shoulders and looked him in the eye.

"Kevin, you're in no shape to be running around. You have access to Hartley's office? Good, but you'll have to call and give him the bad news. Stay here and contact NYPD. Get in touch with Staten Island and Westchester, Putnam County, too. Make sure they look for a boat. You'll be our communication hub. We'll keep in touch whenever we can grab a phone booth. Right now we're going to comb the area one more time."

They crossed the square again. No pirates. Sun Ra had finished, and the crowd was thinning out.

"Artemis, let's canvass MacDougal one more time and then check back with Macduff."

Artemis yawned.

"Tunde, any chance we could stop for tea at Caffe Reggio? It looks like this is going to be a long night. I'm too jittery for coffee, but tea would keep me on an even keel. We might get lucky and pick up his trail there."

"I second that motion. Let's go."

They grabbed a small table for two in the crowded cafe. Artemis, in her fashion, began studying the menu in detail, holding it close in the dim light. Ayotunde grew restless.

"Fletch, you order for both of us while I run across the street and check the Kettle of Fish."

Artemis nodded without interrupting her perusal of the menu. There was a great variety of teas, many with flavored infusions. She didn't look up when the waiter approached.

"Hmm. We'll take a pot of…let's see…the apricot tea. Two cups, please."

The order placed, Artemis put down the menu and scanned the room. Dim light and smoke made it hard to discern features clearly. Centuries-old Italian oil portraits brooded over the scene.

With Ayotunde doing a bit of surveillance across the street, Artemis took the opportunity to visit the tiny restroom, leaving her jacket on the back of her chair to mark her turf. As she wove through the tightly packed tables, a flash of chrome in the darkness caught her eye. In the corner was a massive espresso machine. It dominated an entire wall. There were pipes and spigots protruding everywhere. What grabbed Artemis's attention was simply that it bore the unmistakable patina of old Italian craft. That tweaked her historian's instinct, and she spent a few minutes examining it before she continued on to the restroom.

When she returned to her seat, the teapot had arrived. Two cups were filled, one in front of each of the two chairs on either side of the table. The tea was steeping in the cups, and the apricot fragrance from the pot was strong, even overwhelming the musty bouquet of the old café. Tired and revolving the events of the evening in her mind, Artemis let her guard down to enjoy a moment of mental rest. Leaving her jacket hanging on the chair back, she sat down and took her first sip.

CHAPTER 45

MISSING

Ayotunde scanned the crowd at the Kettle of Fish. No pirates. She crossed the street back to Caffe Reggio and made her way to what she distinctly recalled was their table. Artemis's jacket hung on the back of an empty chair. Ayotunde could see that the door of the tiny café restroom was open, so Artemis wasn't in there. A teapot and two cups, one empty and the other half full, stood on the table. Ayotunde made a quick decision to use her newly acquired detective skill. She picked up the teapot and sniffed it. It was aromatic, more so than just black tea. It smelled like dried fruit, but it wasn't the pear smell that would signal chloral hydrate. She sniffed the half empty teacup, and recoiled. Something wasn't right. She ventured another sniff, and this time she made a positive ID. It was the pear smell, the smell from Macduff's rum bottle. So the pot was okay but the cup had been tampered with. The strong fruit smell from the pot must have obscured the hint of pear in the teacup. Whoever did it was experienced at the game. That would be the same person who drugged Macduff; Calico Jack.

Ayotunde looked around the darkened room. There was a surreal quality to the shadowy figures of costumed revelers. She fought off a hint of panic. If Artemis had been kidnapped, there wasn't time to waste on that. Ayotunde was on her own, a novice sleuth with a very real case to crack.

She closed her eyes and quickly compiled a mental list of tasks she needed to do right away. First on the list was to notify Macduff. She dropped a dollar bill on the table and walked quickly out onto MacDougal street.

She raced up a block, crossed through Washington Square Park, and sprinted the last five blocks to the Salmagundi Club. The unlocked front door opened readily, and she found her way to the office. Hartley was sitting at his desk, his head in his hands. She filled them in, breathlessly, on the events of the last half hour. Macduff took her aside.

"This is personal for me. I promised Hartley I would protect that painting, and I blew it."

Ayotunde didn't have time to nurse his bruised pride.

"Our first priority, Kevin, is to locate Artemis."

Hartley, overhearing them, looked up imploringly.

"We have no choice but to open the doors at one p.m. Sunday. If the Hobart Tyler is missing, my reputation is ruined!"

He cast a baleful glance at Kevin, then turned back to Ayotunde.

"I haven't slept well for weeks, worrying about just this!"

Ayotunde took a deep breath and let it out slowly.

"Yes, the Hobart Tyler, of course, Martin. If we can get it back on the wall by one o'clock Sunday, the show will go on, but we also have a case of kidnapping here."

She turned back to Kevin.

"I've got to get moving. I should be back in Valhalla in an hour, and I'll stay by the phone all night long."

Ayotunde roared up the West Side in the Jeep. Her thoughts raced between the painting and Artemis. Time was critical. Life and death might be hanging in the balance. She knew she would need help, so before heading to the Atalanta estate she made a stop at Sarah Lawrence student housing to pick up Olorin. As they joined the late-night weekend traffic on the Sprain Brook Parkway, Ayotunde reached down and switched the radio off.

"Olorin, Artemis has been kidnapped."

The young girl's eyes widened.

Ayotunde filled her in on the Salmagundi Club, Artemis's disappearance from Caffe Reggio, and the dangerous suspect in question. Olorin listened attentively, asking her to repeat certain details. She frowned.

"Can we do nothing more than wait for the police to find her?"

Ayotunde cleared her throat, keeping her eyes fixed on the winding parkway.

"*Omo*, child. When you used to sneak into the sacred grove to study the sculptures at night, that was a bit like being a secret agent, wasn't it?"

Olorin nodded thoughtfully.

"I guess you could say that."

"Well, let me explain to you what Artemis and I do when we are not in the classroom..."

During the twelve-mile drive to Valhalla, Ayotunde filled Olorin in on various adventures and scrapes, including the mad Irish professor and Artemis's recent encounter with the werewolf.

"I particularly wanted to tell you about that incident over in Italy."

"Because?"

"You know our tenant Faunus, right?"

"Sure. He's very quiet, isn't he?"

"Yes, most of the time. But on the full moon, tomorrow night, for example, he's not quiet. He howls at the moon. That's why I told you the story about Italy."

"So he's…?"

"I don't want to frighten you."

"Frighten me! Tunde, I grew up in the forests of Yorubaland, and you know that we firmly believe that souls can migrate to the bodies of animals. This just makes me feel a closer kinship with Faunus!"

Ayotunde breathed a sigh of relief.

"Well, keep in mind that a wolf pack is matriarchal. The males look to an alpha female for direction, and since Faunus is a lone wolf, we are the only pack he has, so he will be docile with us. The full moon rises tomorrow night, and I need to ask a special favor of you, my Yoruba little sister."

Ayotunde outlined the favor as they pulled off onto the side road leading to the estate. Once inside the gates, she knocked on the door of the back cottage.

"Faunus, it's Tunde. Olorin is here, and we need to make a plan."

In the kitchen, she convened a war room. She told her two compatriots everything she knew and emphasized that they were dealing with a criminal who was not just crazy but also dangerous, and he had Artemis in captivity somewhere. They needed to be ready to move at a moment's notice, but until they got some word from Macduff, there was nothing they could do but sit tight.

"Try to get some sleep. Tomorrow will be a busy day."

She turned to Faunus.

"I know that the full moon rises tomorrow at six, but there can be no sequester for you in the quarry this month. We need you if we're going to rescue Artemis."

"She rescued me, twice. Just tell me what you need."

"When Artemis is located, we need to get moving quickly, and if we're in the middle of a rescue when the full moon rises, it will be two women and a wolf in the Jeep. I want you to have extra clothes packed. We could be on her trail for longer than a night and a day, so you will need to be able to transition. Olorin and I know your special needs, Faunus, and we understand. Just trust us as the alpha females in the pack."

CHAPTER 46

THE RITUAL

The following day, October 29th, was an agonizing sequence of snail-paced hours with no word. The autumn shadows were growing long when the telephone rang. It was Macduff.

"We think we might have a bead on him. A Westchester highway patrol chopper spotted a boat tethered to an off-limits island fifty miles up the Hudson from the city."

"Is it a Chris-Craft, flying the skull and crossbones?"

Macduff was startled.

"How did you know that?"

"The pirate who slipped you the knockout drops, his name is Calico Jack. He's not a pirate. He's John Rackham, a delusional mobster. That's his boat. He hides it under an abandoned pier on the waterfront at Chelsea."

"Well, right now it's moored at..."

"Bannerman Castle."

"You know the place?"

"Yes, and I know that if a dozen police boats come roaring up the river, Rackham, or whatever his real name is, could light a single match and set off enough dynamite to literally turn the tide. I'll give you the whole history sometime, but for now you just have to trust me. Have police boats heave-to downriver at Stony Point Lighthouse, and upriver at Saugerties Lighthouse. He'll be trapped. But Kevin, you have to let me and my team go in surgically and get Artemis out."

"I'll get the noose in place. I'll trust you to tighten it. Let me make some calls."

Macduff called back at five o'clock.

"Ayotunde, this is Kevin. The police boats are situated. I've got a high-speed interceptor moored at Cold Spring. There's a phone booth at the marina. Whenever you are ready, I can ferry you out to the island. It's just me; no flashing lights or bullhorns. You're in charge of the rescue."

"On it, Kevin. Give me ninety minutes and we'll meet you at the Cold Spring dock."

She hung up.

"Game on. Everyone in the Jeep. We're taking a hike. Olorin, pack a couple of flashlights, a pair of gloves, and Artemis's buck knife. Toss this in too, for good luck."

She handed her Gae Bolg, the Irish spearhead from Ross Castle.

"Faunus, we know that the moon is full tonight, but that will work in our favor. You will be our strongest ally. I will give you direction with eye contact, and Olorin will as well. We'll work as a team, all for one and one for all. Let's get moving!"

During the forty-five minute drive north, Ayotunde sketched out the plan, with the caveat that everything could change depending on their unpredictable quarry. When they reached Hudson Highlands Park she pulled the Jeep off the road at the

Breakneck Ridge trailhead, the same spot where they had hiked with Artemis during the summer. The trail went straight up, over a thousand feet in a one-mile trek, over rocky ridges left by an old mine. Ayotunde, Olorin, and Faunus were silent, concentrating on their footing in the twilight as they climbed. At the peak, Olorin put down the duffel bag and took a drink from her canteen. Faunus began to twitch, and his breathing quickened. He stretched and strained at his clothing, and his eyes took on a telltale yellow patina. Without a word, he walked into the woods as the glow of the full moon spread across the clearing.

Ayotunde walked to the cliff side above the river and focused her binoculars on the island castle below. In the fading light, she could see the boat moored to the off-limits sign. The walls of the ruin didn't betray any occupants, but there was no doubt in her mind.

When she rejoined her companions, the moon was up. Olorin was sitting on the trunk of a long-fallen oak. She was gently stroking Faunus-as-wolf behind the ears.

"You two seem to be getting along fine. Remember what I told you, Olorin. Wolf packs are matriarchal, and Faunus has been living with me and with Artemis for months now. He is waiting for direction from us. Now, *omo*, I need your help, child. We have a ritual to perform and a short time to do it."

She reached into her backpack and drew out a bundle of sage and a small frame drum with a goatskin head. She laid Gae Bolg, the Irish spearhead, on the ground to her left. Then she lit the sage to make a smudge and handed the drum to Olorin. The younger woman began softly beating the rhythm of the *babalawo*, opening the channel of communication to the *orishas*, the spiritual helpers. Ayotunde closed her eyes and began to chant in a hushed voice. The wolf lay quietly at her feet. She placed her right hand on the creature's head and began to speak in a disembodied voice.

"Osun, river goddess and *orisha*, we beseech you to grant us your protection. Tonight we cross a broad river. Your servant Faunus, a worshipper of you in your moon aspect, is held captive by a *jumbee*, a wayward spirit of the departed, trapped within him but longing to continue on to its place of rest. You have taught us that the *jumbee* cannot cross a river. Guide your servant Faunus and give him strength, that he and the lost spirit may find mutual freedom when they reach the far bank. We beseech you and offer you this burning sage as our sacrifice."

She sat on the rocky ground for a few moments, looking exhausted. Suddenly she opened her eyes and stood up, revived. She stamped out the glowing smudge.

"Let's go."

The two women led the wolf down the steep slope as the last light faded in the forest shade. Ayotunde and Olorin climbed into the front seats of the Jeep and pointed the wolf toward the back. He bounded in, and Ayotunde gunned the Jeep south on Highway 90 toward the Cold Spring dock.

CHAPTER 47

THE CROSSING

With the team onboard, Macduff nursed the interceptor slowly upriver, keeping the diesel growl to a murmur. Ayotunde, Olorin, and the wolf looked straight ahead, in a shared state of heightened awareness as they steamed toward certain danger. As the craft passed the idling police boats at Stony Point, Macduff leaned over toward Ayotunde. He cast his eyes back toward the wolf.

"That animal. Is it..."

"Don't worry about him. He's no threat to you, and he's in my care, so you just concentrate on getting us onto the island without alerting Rackham."

They pulled up at the off-limits placard, where the runabout was tethered. There was no sign of life, but the chain link and barbed wire security fence had been cut and left curled open. Ayotunde touched the spearhead and thought back to the "grateful dead" story that Shane Whelan related in Dublin. The hero had to enter a haunted castle to rescue a princess from the Otherworld. She felt like she had become the heroine of the same story, but without the aid of a magic cloak and sword. What she had, though, was Olorin and the wolf, brave companions.

They stepped ashore.

Macduff kept watch on the quietly idling boat while Ayotunde led Olorin and the wolf, creeping step by step, into the outer chamber of the ruined castle.

CHAPTER 48

THE CAPTIVE

Artemis woke. She was sitting, unable to stand, in a dark, musty space, with dim light coming from somewhere off to the side. She felt solid ground beneath her. A thick rope was tied around her belly, fastening her to something large and heavy behind her back. Her eyes adapted to the darkness, and she looked around. She seemed to be in a canyon, a canyon constructed of wooden crates, painted olive drab. It was some sort of warehouse. She could make out labels, stenciled in yellow paint, on some of the crates.

1200 COUNT .300 CALIBER

1200 COUNT .50 CALIBER

She was imprisoned in an ammunition dump, a massive one. Now she knew where she was: Bannerman Castle.

The light started to dance and move closer, and suddenly she was blinded by it.

"Anne Bonny! I never lost faith that we would be reunited someday. The bloody redcoats strung me up on Gallows Point, and they hung my lifeless body in the cruel gibbet where every sailor entering Port Royal could mock me, but here I am, and here you are on this worthy square-rigger, moored at world's end. Together we'll hoist the Jolly Roger once again and lay waste to any merchant ship foolish enough to come crosswise!"

For the first time since they met at the Cedar Tavern, she saw Calico Jack Rackham's face in the light of the battery lantern he set down on a crate marked in yellow stencil 1200 COUNT .45 CALIBER.

He lit a cigar, then blew out the match and put it in his vest pocket.

"Mustn't be careless out here, Annie. One false strike of the match and our ship would go up like a bonfire on Guy Fawkes Day. No, we've got other plans for these munitions, these millions of shells and canisters of black powder. Calico Jack and Anne Bonny, the king and queen of pirates! Take a look at this, my lovely."

He pulled a parcel out of his shoulder bag and unwrapped the thumb box painting. He admired it in the lantern light.

"Pretty little picture, I daresay. A pretty little picture worth millions. With this in our possession, we become the king and queen, and King George will sleep with one eye open for fear of our reach!"

He set the painting down next to the lantern.

What the madman was calling his ship was actually an island of surplus wartime ammunition, and Artemis was tied down on it with a sailor's figure-of-eight. The stronger she strained against it, the more the knot tightened.

Artemis watched as Rackham busied himself. He uncoiled a length of rope and tied one end to a barrel stave behind her head. He walked out of the stone chamber, trailing the rope behind him. A few minutes later, he reentered with a paintbrush and a one-gallon gasoline can.

Still singing to himself in a merry voice, he decanted a small amount of fuel into a bucket and dipped the paintbrush in. Still singing, he drew the brush along the length of rope, disappearing once again out of the chamber door. He was making a fuse.

CHAPTER 49

THE PROPHECY

Rackham continued his deadly puttering about. He quaffed liberally on a bottle of white rum, and his tongue began to loosen to an even greater extent than his normal barrage of boastfulness.

"Ann, my lovely, the bloody lime-juicers will never take us alive, not while I'm captain of this brigantine."

"What makes you so sure?"

"The fortune teller in Washington Square sprinkled beans on a tin plate. He recited some mumbo-jumbo and then looked me in the eye. He told me directly that I died once at the hands of the redcoats and their white-wigged judge, but it would never happen again. I'll never again feel the hangman's noose, never be hung up in the infernal gibbet, and you, my lovely, will never rot with the rats in their jail again. The witch doctor told me so."

"So he said you were immortal? You think that if you light that fuse we will somehow survive?"

"Survive? No! If the limeys board this ship, I will strike my last match and we will all go together to Davy Jones's locker."

He quaffed deeply from the bottle of rum.

"But they won't hang me."

He wiped his lips on his sleeve.

"Mark these words, my sweet. When the witch doctor was done, I pressed a silver dollar in his hand. He grabbed me by the wrist and said, 'Beware the dire wolf.' Then he packed off into the throng. So you see…"

He upended the bottle, drained the last drop, and with his head still thrown back, he bellowed: "I have no creature on Earth to fear, save the dire wolf. Jacktars and judges be damned!"

He stiffened suddenly and quickly doused the lantern. Something rustled in the outer chamber.

CHAPTER 50

THE PURSUIT

Ayotunde and Olorin crouched in the dark, listening to the strange conversation on the other side of the stone wall. Olorin had already used the buck knife to sever the rope in several places, rendering it useless as long as they could somehow overcome Rackham before he could strike his match.

Ayotunde looked down at the wolf. Their eyes met, and she reminded herself that he awaited direction from the alpha female. She touched Gae Bolg for luck, gestured toward the inner chamber, and whispered, "Go."

The wolf trotted into the chamber with fangs bared. At the sound of his growl, Rackham flicked the lantern back on, and the blood drained out of his face.

"Dear god. The dire wolf."

He fell down onto his knees.

"Blood of Christ, I've killed many an innocent man and sent them to their eternal reward. Don't send me now to my fiery fate. Let me retire to the cloister!"

The wolf softly padded closer to him and growled again.

"I'll make a pilgrimage to the Holy Land, on my knees! Just take this monstrous apparition from my sight!"

Seeing that his entreaties were falling on deaf ears in heaven, Calico Jack panicked. He sprang past the wolf and bolted out of the chamber, leaving Artemis to her fate at the jaws of the dire wolf. He pushed past Ayotunde and Olorin, shouting that they would never condemn him for a second time to the gallows. His last match, never struck, lay next to the empty rum bottle where he had dropped it in his frenzy to escape.

The two women untied Artemis and embraced her, while the wolf followed the would-be pirate king in hot pursuit. Rackham leapt into the cockpit of the runabout and gunned the motor, shouting, "Let the devil's horse race begin!"

He threw the runabout into gear and raced upriver while the wolf howled onshore in the moonlight. Nearby on the idling interceptor, Macduff watched him go but didn't pursue. That would mean abandoning his three companions on an island that might explode at any moment. He breathed a sigh of relief when Ayotunde emerged from the ruins, holding the unharmed Hobart Tyler painting. She was followed by Olorin steadying a groggy Artemis, also unharmed, on her arm. All present and accounted for, they boarded the interceptor, and Macduff guided it slowly out to mid-river, then opened the throttle.

He shouted to Ayotunde over the engine's roar, "I figure he can squeeze thirty knots out of that old Chris-Craft. Wide open, this interceptor can do fifty. He's not getting away this time."

Macduff was ashamed of his poor performance as night watchman down at the Salmagundi Club, and he was determined to make up for it. They were passing Hyde Park when the interceptor's searchlight found the Chris-Craft.

"Olorin, keep that light trained on his stern. Don't follow him too closely, though. He's going to run into trouble. Keep that life preserver ready in case we need to fish him out of the drink."

Showered with spray but keeping his eyes on the river, he shouted to Ayotunde, "Back during the Revolution, Washington's troops planted obstacles in the Hudson to impede the British navy. They used a device called the *cheval-de-frise*. It was a frame dumped in the river with sharpened spikes aiming toward the surface. Some of them are still there. They're indicated on the navigational charts, but I have a feeling Rackham is not looking at any charts right now. He's going to be wide of the safe channel."

Saugerties lighthouse extends like a small peninsula from the west bank of the Hudson, almost to the middle of the river. Three police boats were idling with lights out across the open channel. As Rackham approached the lighthouse, Macduff shouted into his radio and the police turned on their spotlights. In the glare, the Chris-Craft was bouncing like a cracking whip on the surface of the river as its mad captain, abandoning any caution, veered toward the lighthouse, looking for a way to evade the interceptors. Macduff shook his head.

"Here we go."

As if on cue, the Chris-Craft, outside the safe channel, struck the point of a centuries-old *cheval-de-frise* with a thunderous crack. The hull started coming apart. Rackham was shaking his fist in the air like a mad Captain Ahab when the boat hit the island at full speed. The splintered hull overturned, jettisoning its lone occupant onto the rocks. He lay still while Macduff slowed and approached the Coast Guard dock.

Olorin jumped ashore to catch the rope and secure it to a cleat. At that moment, the inert Rackham suddenly came back to life. Unafraid, Olorin pulled the buck knife from its sheath and blocked the narrow bridge to the mainland. The pirate, a trapped rat, yanked open the lighthouse door and vanished inside. Not knowing if he was armed, the colleagues stopped at the foot of the stairway. Ayotunde looked down at the wolf, and then glanced upward. He raced up the stairway, howling in a lupine battle call. They followed him up the stairs, where they found him, fangs bared, keeping guard over a trembling Rackham, who was still supplicating the heavens, to no avail.

A police boat was dispatched to steam full speed downriver to the pier at Chelsea, where the painting could be safely returned to the Salmagundi gallery. Another boat carried the handcuffed Calico Jack to his entry into the criminal justice system. There was one more task at hand before the sun rose.

CHAPTER 51

THE BROKEN SPELL

It was time to cross the narrow bridge to the west bank of the Hudson, where Saugerties police and rescue vehicles waited to debrief the rescuers and transport them home. As they crossed the bridge, Ayotunde whispered a prayer.

"Osun, river goddess. We have crossed the opalescent river. Please remember our entreaty to release the *jumbee* from his captivity, that he may journey onward, and your servant Faunus will be set free."

On the mainland, Ayotunde tossed Faunus's knapsack into a grove of scrub oaks. She turned to the wolf. Their eyes met again, and she glanced into the grove. The wolf obediently followed her glance, tail down. She joined Artemis and Macduff at the parking area beyond the trees, where they were processed and declared fit to return home. As the sun rose on the eastern horizon, Frank Faunus emerged from the oak grove, dressed in his khakis.

"I don't know how I got here, but..."

He looked around at a trio of smiling faces amid a clutch of emergency vehicles and swirling lights.

"I have a feeling it's probably best to let the mystery be."

CHAPTER 52

THE PERIPATETIC PAINTING

Promptly at one o'clock in the afternoon Martin Hartley threw open the doors of the Grand Gallery.

"Ladies and gentlemen, as president of the Salmagundi Club, I am proud to welcome you once again to our annual thumb box exhibition. Before we take down the velvet rope, I want to dedicate this year's show to our departed member, the distinguished Hobart Tyler. It gives me great pleasure to announce that this year we have a special treat for you, the first ever viewing of his *Bear Mountain at Sunset*, a priceless addition to our thumb box collection."

As the crowd of art connoisseurs surged past him into the gallery, Hartley glanced over at Macduff, took a deep breath, and mopped his brow.

"That was too close for comfort."

Macduff patted him on the shoulder.

"You know the old saying, Martin. All's well that ends well. Hey, is the tap still flowing downstairs? I think we could both use a libation."

CHAPTER 53

THE LINGERING MYSTERY

Back at Atalanta, on a chilly November morning, Artemis and Ayotunde were relaxing over coffee. John Coltrane's *Meditations* was on the turntable.

"You know, Artemis, there is something about that case that still puzzles me."

She took a sip and put down her mug.

"We're professors, we've got a campus library, and we know from history that there was a real John Rackham, a pirate who called himself Calico Jack. We also know that the object of his affection was Anne Bonny. And we know that Rackham was hung in Jamaica, and Anne Bonny vanished from the pages of history."

"Yes?"

"Well, my point is that we know all that from books, but the Calico Jack that we just captured grew up on the streets, and I just can't picture him poring over dusty volumes at the New York Public Library. If we discount that, how does he know what he knows? How did he acquire his name, and why does he search for Anne Bonny?"

Artemis pursed her lips thoughtfully.

"Tunde, there's one lesson in this strange profession that keeps coming back to me."

"And that is…?"

"Sometimes we just need to let the mystery be."

CHAPTER 54

THE TOAST

Around a table at John's Pizza on Bleecker Street, the four adventurers were distributing slices according to favorite toppings. Artemis stood and proposed a toast.

"I want to thank all of you for saving me from spending eternity in the afterlife as a pirate queen!"

"Hear, hear!"

"And I especially want to thank Olorin, our newest team member! Faunus, we've come a long way from the lemon groves of Amalfi, haven't we? For one thing, you're eating here at John's instead of waiting tables, and thanks to Ayotunde and the protective *orishas*, you no longer need to hide away under the full moon. In fact..."

She paused, portentously.

"I invited Dido Parren to my lecture at Sarah Lawrence next Saturday, and she told me she couldn't make it because..." Artemis looked around the table with a conspiratorial grin. "She has a date for dinner and a movie...with you!"

Faunus's face matched the red checks on the tablecloth as his newfound friends slapped him on the back. Artemis's grin grew even wider.

"And now…" She raised her glass of house red. "Here's to pizza and more adventures!"

They clinked glasses all around.

www.ingramcontent.com/pod-product-compliance
Lightning Source LLC
LaVergne TN
LVHW050639100826
845148LV00011B/1914